Duce Kingdom

Efualajong Folefac

Langaa Research & Publishing CIG
Mankon, Bamenda

Publisher:
Langaa RPCIG
Langaa Research & Publishing Common Initiative Group
P.O. Box 902 Mankon
Bamenda
North West Region
Cameroon
Langaagrp@gmail.com
www.langaa-rpcig.net

Distributed in and outside N. America by African Books Collective
orders@africanbookscollective.com
www.africanbookcollective.com

ISBN: 9956-791-37-7

DISCLAIMER
All views expressed in this publication are those of the author and do
not necessarily reflect the views of Langaa RPCIG.

Dedication

I dedicate this book to my lovely mum, Anyingoh Esther and my late dad, Efualajong Tatuh Stephen whose demise had been felt by every member of the family. To my lovely daughter, Esther Folefac whose loving smiles has given me a lot of inspiration.

My appreciation goes to my alma mater-Presbyterian comprehensive secondary school Buea, for building the foundation of education through to my parent educatory; the University of Buea, which have led to what I am today. To Ayealefac Kejang and his family, for being there for me when all hope seemed to have been lost. To Tazisong Christopher and his family for putting me back to track when I seemed to have lost my way. To all my mates and colleagues, especially Christopher Finch and Albert Somi Cyril for their candy and friendship, that was spiced with lots of humour. To my beloved mum and siblings, for their support and encouragement. Most importantly, to you my readers, for liking my book and buying a copy and not pirating it. I hold you all close to my heart.

About the Author

I was born in a small village call Muyenge which situates in the southwest region of Cameroon. Their major produce are cocoa, cocoyams, plantain and other cash crops. The economy in this village is very booming but they lack roads and other facilities to transport their crops to the market. I went through my nursery and primary school in this village before moving to Buea where I completed the rest of my education.

I'm blessed with my precious mum, Anyingoh Esther who worked hard enough to see me through school together with my siblings after the demise of my father in 2001. In 2011, I published my first book titled Narrow Mistake with Xlibris cooperation in the USA.

About the book

Duce Kingdom is a compelling mythical story of magic, sacrilege and violence, written in fine style of both the first and third person dialogue and narration. The story commenced with the rage of darkness that poised the land through to the official inauguration of the king, their frustrations due to the tightness of their laws for kingdom sake and tradition, which had shattered their freedom. The Sacrifices of virgins they made to their gods, wars, romance and beheadings of criminals, which made their future almost uncertain. The story continues with the blending of the old and ancient evil and black magic from the forgotten corners of the planet that throbbed and how they resisted-the yesteryears of tradition and how it saw its revolution by the birth of a powerful sorcerer, Zalinda who redeemed the kingdom from its woes.

Chapter 1

The new age
Rage of darkness

Sleep was meant to rest the bones and refresh the flesh-dreams to go beyond imaginations, to somewhere in the empty; for fun, omen and ancestral blessings, where fantasies in the realms were reverted to realities, making the impossible possible in the world of wonders. Not this age, not this land called Duce kingdom.

It was close to night, the cloud quickly paraded the sky, saluting the land, bathing the atmosphere and reminding the sun to end its shift and go to sleep. No one knew why, no one could explain, nature had made it clear and reserved its explanations, scheduling every darkness and light to enchant the hours, and hide the unseen from hurting humans. Not this time, the temple bells rang alarming with intimidation; very loud, reminding the indigenes that night was at hand. They were at the squares of all the cities, villages and towns going about with their businesses. Three masquerades trotted past everywhere in the cities, sending the indigenes into their homes.

Then came from somewhere beyond, somewhere above the realms of empty and along the horizon, a billow of darkness which covered the land in thick fog of an angry weather. Like allies, a strong and violent storm went across Duce sweeping every loose mass and putting off all the candles that lit the land in fury. No one had any choice, not even the queen Josephine and they resorted to resting in the comfort of their beds sleeping. A voice whispers from

1

somewhere in the dark cloud chanting sleeping spells. It flew through the land in dark winds sniffed by everybody in Duce. They went into a deep sleep and dreams took their souls to wonder land-to a mystery not yet discovered. In this dream, the air began echoing the earth's squeak and above the atmosphere were series of screeches all massing down their noises deep into their ears; this *pow* threatened the moon not to reflect its light to prove its seriousness and was stern about it. They were deep at sleep and the realities were taking place in the form of a dream.

It was not over just yet and the memories were still deep in the minds of the gods memories of how humans had ventured challenging them in the old age. Something they were bound never to forget, something they were never to erase from their minds - the shame humans brought on their very existence. It was time for payback, the time when the gods had decided to smile over human miseries, making them to realise they were supreme and commanded the universe - especially the people of Duce whose history was based on sacrilege.

A heavy thunder stroke cracking through the earth crust and a torrential rain fell, flooding every region. From beneath came huge bubbles never seen anywhere in the land-produced by some creatures.

From their sleep, their souls left their bodies wondering in a world they knew not, made of shadows and dark blue spheres-a strange land as they thought but indeed, it was Duce. The queen saw herself just descending down from an avalanched mountain, from a heavy permeation with her knights in a bloody looking frost; yet, their swords were still very firm in their hands ready to engage in any threatening issues. From nowhere came whooshing a powerful *mana* that flushed down to the cracks the thunder had created. From

2

beneath came a legion of powerful and dangerous demons called the *Splimiide*, making their way to the surface of the earth like ants when disturbed in their habitat, very skinny, hungry and thirsty. Above were their friends descending below like vultures, the queen and her knights drew backward, noticing the demons from a distance in their ugly, thorny and frightful physiology much of a bastard caricature peeking at them. The queen stepped forward, ran through her hair with her fingers in disbelief and stretched her hands sideways putting them in a halt. She then bent at kneel level squinting and peeking at the *Splimiide*, calculating the distance to note how much time they were left to prepare themselves. The way they stood was unfriendly and it did not take a guess to think they were some form of an enemy to them.

'Prepare your armour, tie your boots and sharpen your swords, I sense danger, the gods are raged and they are coming for us, look,' she pointed at the direction to which the *Splimiide* stood,

'The angels of the holy darkness,' said Josephine

'Angels of the holy darkness!' they all exclaimed

'Do any of you know anything about them?' she asked scanning at them all.

One of the knights called Armand, stepped forward,

'I'm not sure my queen, but I've read stories about them in the library of *Elmscot* in Fontem, they're creatures of dark magic, from the underworld. Also, from prophecies which were encrypted on the walls of the libraries in cuneiform-confirming the coming of the *Splimiide* to revenge what humans did to the gods in the forgotten age.' said Armand, walking towards the queen.

'The age of your father my queen,' he whispered with his sword firm

The queen gazed at him and scanned the rest of the knights again for some minutes, 'We'll face them, we'll fight for our lives and save the kingdom of Duce from the hands of bloody enemies called gods,' said the queen, in a solemn voice .

Duce had been their chosen quay and their discontentment in harbouring there had led to a scrimmage between humans and the demons. At once, they took their shield closer to them and threatened to march in their direction, something else crossed the queen's mind, 'Halt,' she cried aloud. They turned and looked at her; she gazed at them with her mouth shaking, as if panicked by the temperament of her view.

'Today may be a day of no return; today may be a day of destiny. I want you all to know that, no matter what happens, you'll all be treated as queens and kings, the true sons and daughters of the land,' She paused for a minute, bent her head down, raised it up quickly, looked straight to the heavens and raised her sword very high up and shouted;

'For the kingdom, for the kingdom,' she shouted out loudly glancing at the sky, 'For the kingdom, life's like death, death like life, we owe it to the kingdom to protect the land of Duce, huaaaaa!' The knights all replied raising their swords ten times higher than she had previously raised hers with enthusiasm in fighting for Duce. The queen led them taking them behind a mountain where they could hide and peep at the *Splimiide* and devise a strategy on how to attack them.

The *Splimiide* were very viable and awry but still looking hungry; they lay down on their bellies, closed their eyes, and appeared to be resting but deep in their minds outrageous thoughts raged on how to feed on the queen and her knights whom they had seen from afar. Though they pretended to sleep, the queen and her knights were very careful and safeguarded themselves-tip-toeing closer to the *Splimiide* to have a full look at their ugliness. About thirty metres to where they slept, the *Splimiide*'s stomachs rumbled so loudly that it brought out the fear in them and they backed off scared of waking them up. The place where they slept was very smelly, not good enough for them to breath in the air around because of its unsavoury nature. They pulled out a small cotton cloth fastened somewhere along their belt tied around their loin to keep their armour in position and covered their noses to reduce the intensity of the musty and decaying air they were sniffing. One of them opened its right eye eyeing them wickedly as they went closer and silently adjusted its posture, sighting and trapping them but tried to remain calm and go unnoticed, while the others went to sleep unnoticed. As they approached, this particular *Splimiide* contracted its body ready to spring and grip their flesh for food but they were very slow in their advance and its patience was burning-eager to fill its flaccid stomach with their fine bodies. It jumped and gripped the neck of one of the knights.

"ah-uhh-ooh-ha"

The knight cried aloud flicking his hands to get rid of the *Splimiide* that had gotten hold of him. The rest of the knights together with the queen carried him quickly away from the presence of the other demons sealing his mouth with their palms to prevent him making more noise and fully waken up the rest of the demons. When they arrived the back of the mountain, they laid him down the queen reached for her dagger, pierced through the *Splimiide* and each knight struggled to land a blow, even those far from him. Above the atmosphere were other invincible demons- a special form of the *Splimiide*, they were watching the humans ill-treating one of their own. They waited patiently hoping it would fight back and cause destruction. As they waited, they never saw any reaction to impress them but noticed the silence of one of the demons. Death was not what they came to face from the hands of humans; their mission was to kill, so, in anger, they flew downward with maximum speed hopping to sweep out the group of humans they were seeing. From afar, one of the knights heard their flapping wings, and looked upward and saw them. 'Run' he cried out loudly.

Everyone was confused at first and thought the sleeping demons were now awake, they reached out quickly to their swords while running haphazardly away from the sleeping demons, he cried out again, 'Not the sleeping *Splimiide*, their accomplices above us,' as they were running;

'What?' they questioned.

They all looked up, searching through the sky as fast as they could with their heads up, they saw the flying demons hunting down on them. They stopped abruptly, ganged themselves up as a crowd, looking straight to the direction above where the demons were descending-holding their swords, spears and shields very firm in their hands. At the order of the queen, they were to defend themselves. She was somewhere at the centre of their midst and could only be identified by her specially made helmet she wore on her head; usually red and patchily coloured sky blue.

'Hold, hold,' the queen ordered and they held their shields tight.

The *Splimiide* in their maximum speed, descended closer to prey on them- came near to fulfil point, and the queen ordered,

'Defend.'

At once, they all raised their shields, covering their heads like roofs and the demons rained on them. The force with which they hit their shields forced them a few centimetres into the earth and bending and twisting and squashing their shields, which was made of thin layer of iron. Some of the demons died while some had nasty injuries; breaking their arms, wings and legs while others were very fine. All cried loudly and the noise woke up the sleeping *Splimiide*. They immediately rushed to where they heard their friends crying coming closer to the queen and her knights with full force.

'This is not going to be good,' cried the queen. At once, she gave orders, 'Attack'.

No single man was left standing, they all reached out to every weapon they had, facing the *Splimiide*, fighting fiercely. Thousands of knights were dying and the *Splimiide* had the advantage, killing and preying on them; tearing through them with their sharp and long claws. Everywhere was bathed with the blood of wounded knights and Splimiide, their nerves became unstable and adrenaline rose, energy burning low but the many of the *Splimiide* were still untouched, attacking hard with great intentions of wiping out the indigenes of Duce. The gods were silently watching at their orientation that was so feeble. Humans had wanted to live a free life without a true supreme, and, the gods were determined in laughing loudly at them. To them, even if the gods had wronged humans, there were better ways of solving the woes rather than riot and violence bringing curses upon their own selves- they could have prayed for mercy and begged the gods for favour, so the gods had hoped, but it went out differently. Humans are now trapped by the mistake of the past, the indigenes had all been indoctrinated to believing there was nothing like god and the gods were angry. They wanted humans to be realistic and recognise that, a supreme being exists, and they are nothing without a supreme being. Which of course the people of Duce hated the word supreme, they had been through many hard times caused by the gods, killing and savaging their innocent citizens.

The queen and her knights were feeling the pressure and in trying to defend themselves, the *Splimiide* kept pushing them in a rough attack to eliminate them at the top of the mountain. When they realised they were half way on the climb trying to defend themselves, the queen winked at them, for them to rush into the *Splimiide* attacking boldly with the little energy they had for them to escape to a nearby cave at the foot of the mountain-the Crain cave. They descended with full force, waging, pushing and cutting through any *Splimiide* that stood on their way, making their way through to the foot of the mountain into the cave. When they had fully entered the cave, they rolled a large stone at the mouth of the cave and closed the cave. The cave was vibrating caused by the pounding of their hearts and their vibrating and wobbly legs. They stood panting, bending with some of the knights holding their waist, wiggling and feeling the pains of war.

From all corners, they searched through to see if they could see any standing water to be able to have a sip and quench their thirst. Nothing as such was at the corner, their throats were dried and their queen was severely dehydrated, lying at one corner helplessly praying for death. They all watched her with pity glancing at each other. Armand dug a stone from the ground and used his dagger to carve a deep hole in it, then uses his cloth to clean the stone, then, spat a thick and almost moisture-less saliva on to the carved stone and passed it round to all the knights. They all did the same until it was full to brim, they gave it to Armand, he took it, rose from his seated position, went to the queen, knelt before her and gave her the saliva for her to drink and regain some little water in her body. She collected it, scanned at them all with her dying-sleepy eyes and gradually taking the stone of saliva into her mouth. The former king of Duce in order to protect his warriors from the gruesomeness of war and his entire family when situations become unfavourable built the Crain cave. One of the knights was sitting closer to the door leading to an open stream but they did not know, where he sat was a planted rock which was the key to the door, he uprooted it without knowing and the door winded up and they gazed at flowing stream,

'Water,' they shouted out in joy seizing the stone from the hand of the queen and rushing towards the stream to fetch some water for her. When she had finished drinking, they bowed before her and she gave orders to them,

'Drink up, the fountain of water, quench your thirst and regain your strength,' said the queen, and they dived into the stream drinking and some stood at the fountain and drank until their stomachs were topped. They went back into the cave, which was very dusky crowded with spider webs, which they had gotten stuck to their armours, which did not mean anything to them and made a smooth and nice hearth, warming themselves with the heat of the fire and discussing with one another; snapping twigs and throwing them on to the fire. The queen went from one knight to the other inspecting their wounds and bandaging them with the care and great emotion of a caring mother. They were startled, it had never happened in the history of their land for the queen or king to stoop with such courage and show such affection to his/her people the way she was doing, they were gladdened by her care, which brought out great courage from the depth of their hearts to protect and fight for her.

Outside the cave, the *Splimiide* had surrounded the entire mountain searching for possible ways to get in contact with them. Another rumbling echoed very loudly such that they could hear while inside the cave, they turned their heads up, down and around trying to figure out where the sound came from then realised that the demons were the cause. The

Splimiide were out there very hungry and would do anything to eat. They started digging, the more they dug, the more energy they were losing, so, they searched for comfortable positions and slept quietly.

Armand dipped his hand into his small leather bag hung across his shoulder right up to his waist and removed an ancient book which contained the deepest of all the secrets of the kingdom that, even the queen knew not. Armand had been the librarian serving two kings and now the queen but he remained strong and agile, he looked like a man of yesterday. He took the courage in joining the queen's knights so that what happened in the days of her father will not repeat its' self in her age. The two kings had failed, he sees the queen as a destined queen for the kingdom,

'What was it you removed from your bag Armand?' the queen asked curiously, Armand had expected she would definitely ask, 'The book of CHANTALS,' he replied

'What does that mean?' the queen asked.

'My queen,' he started, coughed and cleared his throat, placing his right palm at the centre of his chest and continued, 'I've served two kings, and, words of this book are not to be discussed in the presence of your knights-only before the queen and the queen alone.' Said Armand

'Does it really require such privacy? The queen asked

He gazed at the queen and offered no word.

The queen moved two steps closer to him and looked into his eyes then ordered the rest of the knights,

'Leave us' said the queen authoritatively.

They left to the other section of the cave doing one or two things and only the queen and Armand were in the main cave, he stretched his hand forth to the queen with the book in his hand,

'Take my queen, the book of CHANTALS'

'What does this mean?'

'The words in print of an ancient magician who had prophesied about the woes of this age and wrote what has to be done to stop the woes,'

'Really? How come you never told me this? She asked, stretching her hand towards the book.

'It never occurred to me too my queen but, I must admit, the ancient magicians were very powerful, according to the book, the book and words in it will appear occurring in the brain of the librarian to profess before the queen and her alone on the eve before the Break-day.'

'Break-day?' The queen uttered.

'Yes my queen, the day when death would befall the knights of this kingdom, chaos and tears flowing down the cheek of the mighty and hope threatening to cease. My queen, you need to open the book and go to page sixty eight and read the enchantments with precision, after you have done that, the Staff of *Clehem* would appear on your right side, pick it up and hold it closed to you with care because, that staff will save you and me from the calamity yet to come.'

'What about the rest?' the queen asked

'The staff can only protect two; the mighty and the librarian. That is why; the words were to be said out of the earshot of the rest of the knights. Their lives end here in the Crain cave, but, you gave your word-that they would be treated as queen and kings, so, this cave would be remembered for eternity as the cave where the knights of this kingdom gave their life to free the land from curse,' Said Armand.

The queen opened the page and read the enchantments, a light flashed, and blinded them temporally, then their eyes became clear and the queen turned beside her and saw the

Staff of Clehem, she picked it up closer to her and tears ran down her cheek, Armand turned and backed her-refusing to see her tears.

'I never thought that before my own eyes, I would see the tears of the mighty. The book was somewhere in the interior of the library of Elmscot, I do not know how it got into my bag,' said Armand.

'What next?' the queen asked curiously.

'The staff will protect and lead us to the Gravel land, where we will meet the most powerful sorcerer ever existed in this universe and, we will hand the staff to him and he shall cleanse the curse placed on this land for eternity. His name is Zalinda,'

'Zalinda?' Said the queen.

'The power of yesterday and today, the only man who can mediate with the gods to forgives us, but you must believe my queen, you must believe that true supreme beings exist and the errors of the gods are not to be judged by humans. Only then, shall we be free and the land cleansed for eternity. The journey to the Gravel land is not easy because we will pass through seven camps of deadly magic.' Said Armand

The queen sighed, and threw the staff down and pick up her sword,

'I refused to believe, nothing exists as a supreme being, the gods are a bunch of scavengers wanting to only savage on us humans. You know how many people died in the old age? Millions and more.' She left and stood at one corner restlessly, pacing and at one point, she squatted staring at him. Armand picked the staff and put in his bag.

Pius, one of the knights was hiding, and listening to what they were saying. At once, he jumped into the main cave and pulled out his sword, seized Armand and wanted to chop his head off. The queen intervened and ordered him to drop his sword down, none of the knights knew why he acted like that but the queen immediately sensed he must have overhead them, and, whispered to him to tell no one. The pain of what he had heard them saying was eating his mind up and he sat at his own corner looking very wistful, poking his fingers in and out of the soil trying to distract his mind. Armand went closer to him, tapped his shoulder to calm him down, he shunted him and left his seated position and mingled with the rest of the knights; they stood watching at the strange behaviour he was portraying.

'What could've gone wrong? They wondered in their minds but sat quiet.

At the other end where the queen stood, the knights noticed she was restless; they questioned not but stood watching in silence.

An hour before the *"break-day"*, Pius went before the queen and the rest of the knights, he pinned his sword before her, removed his helmet; then picked up his sword and pierced his stomach, and blood started oozing from the wounded region and from his mouth. 'Why have you decided to bring curse upon this land by taking your own life knight of Duce?' asked the queen.

'Let me go my queen. It is hard to believe that the road we have fought so hard to conquer will end here, the...' said Pius

'...speak no more,' said the queen using her hand to cover the region where the blood was oozing, he knelt down coughing out blood. The knights thought the queen was just stopping him from speaking too much and causing more blood oozing out of his wounded body. She did not want him to expose the little he knows. Armand and some other knights carried him and tried to treat him but failed and he died. The queen was bitter and she knew not when tears ran down her cheek again in agony, every knight wept and they buried him in the cave. When they were through with the burial ceremony, the queen rose and spoke to them.

'My people, my heart is heavy by the woes of the land and I have seen your effort in trying to protect this kingdom, the future of our young generation, but I would like to state, let hunger kill us, let's lose our lives in battle, not using our hands to take our own life whatever the case. If anything troubles you, talk to someone, share your down cast and stop cursing the land by taking your own life.' Said the queen sounding very bitter concerning what Pius had done.

Chapter 2

A few minutes to the "*break-day*", the Staff of Clehem started glowing on and off. Armand walked and stood beside the queen. All of a sudden, the cave started vibrating and collapsed. All the knights were confused and ran from one end to the other. When it became unbearable, some went and rolled off the stone at the mouth of the cave to flee from the disaster, the *Splimiide* were just outside waiting to devour them. They tried to force their way out but the demons would not allow them to, tearing through their flesh and clinging on to them like ants when trampled upon their route. The staff glowed finally and disappeared with the queen and the librarian. The knights were all doomed and the *Splimiide* destroyed and fed on all of them leaving no bones.

The staff took them to a very blur world, dark and dangerous, the sounds of animals kept repeating, every object was angry to be disturbed, and they kept on trampling on them. Every object in the world started hissing echoing in their ears like the sound of a drum playing in a lonely forest. The queen was terribly afraid and clung on to the librarian holding him firm. He removed the staff of clehem and showed it to her, 'Do you now believe?' he asked

The queen pushed it away and it fell down, Armand picked it up and put it in his bag. From behind them, a large dragon with golden eyes appeared his breath like the western winds and his body covered with scales. They heard a strange noise coming from behind them, and turned to look at what was making the noise. They saw the dragon and were stunned; the queen pulled out her sword and pointed at the dragon.

'What do you want and where are you from?' asked the queen boldly but inside her, she was dead cold and had to muster this courage to speak out like a queen.

The dragon gazed at them turning its head left and right with its head down, then, it raised its head up.

'I am the last dragon from the realm of Efianku; the lost land of magic that was cursed by the gods and destroyed by a powerful sorcerer. I've not come to hurt you rather, to protect you.'

'So, you do speak?' asked Armand

'Yes I do speak' said the dragon lying down on its belly.

'For four hundred years, I have watched over the land of Duce, her rising and falling kings, the chaos that went across them and the blood that painted the land. I even wrote the book of *chantals* to save the kingdom but the magicians could not see it-blinded by the spells of the god of war. After the falling of the king in the old age, I decided to choose the librarian to do my bidding and enchanted the staff of clehem to lead you to me so that, I can then fortify your journey to the Gravel land.'

'So, you were the one who killed my knights?'

'It was meant to be so. You see my noble queen, in the beginning the land of Duce was meant to be lost forever cursed by great gods because the greatest of all evil, the most powerful and wicked magician lived there and was conquered. After his death, the gods decided to wipe out this land forever but I decided to protect the land, and, because of this land-which was at that time called Efianku, I was exiled from the planet of the dragons. Luckily enough they did not take my powers away from me. I was afraid they might come back for my powers and do I transferred my powers to the staff of clehem making sure, in case something happened to me the magic in it would help your son Zalinda to be able to cleanse the cursed land of Duce. I feel so happy now, that, my powers have returned to me while I am still alive. As for your knights, they are just a few who have died to save the many.'

The queen was weak after hearing all this, dropped down her sword, went and sat on top of a rock just next to where the dragon was lying. The dragon sniffed in a deep breath and drew the powers from the staff of clehem into his body, his eyes turned green and he said to them,

'I am your staff and the protector to guide you to the Gravel land, your quest to end the curse in the land I hold close to my heart.' said the dragon and he turned again and said to them, 'Follow me.' Like a sheep, they began running behind him to the land of the sorcerer-Zalinda. They walked for a distance of eight miles and he turned and asked the queen, 'Have you changed your hardened heart yet, noble daughter of Duce?'

'What heart?' the queen asked.

'Do you now believe in supreme, that, supreme rule and are the sole protectorate of the land of Duce?' asked the dragon.

She stared at the dragon for a while and went closer to him and scratched her back and said,

'Because of you, I have known what could not have been known and I have seen what could not have been seen, I am just a mere mortal and I think true supreme exist.'

'Fair enough,' said the dragon and Armand stood at one corner praising the sky for touching the queen's mind.

'This makes our journey simpler and less difficult. You see my noble one, you and the inhabitants of Duce are mere mortals and have no right to judge the ways of the gods. Even in the realms of the gods, there are evils and righteousness and kurice was just one of the evil that came to destroy the land. You were misled and betrayed and instead of you praying hard, you went ahead cursing the gods. They decided to turn their back on Duce after I had pleaded with them to show mercy upon the land. They trusted you all for my sake and began to restore the land and you all made a terrible mistake by insulting them, which led to my exile from the land. If you now believe, then things are going to be better and Zalinda the greatest sorcerer of all kind will know what to do.'

The queen coughed, the dragon continued, 'May we now move on, noble one?' and they started trekking, crossing and jumping through fallen tree logs. After they have covered a certain distance, the dragon walked quickly passing them both and stood in front of them. They stopped, and he turned and looked at them and said,

'We are about to enter the Shadow land, if anything happens to me, please continue without me' and he turned and breathed on to them the magic breath on to them which gave them enough powers to defend themselves when needed. The powers went into them and they felt their bodies heating from within as if they were in a blaze. They wiggled, wiggled, and finally came back to normal when their bodies had absorbed the magic given to them by the dragon. The magic was so great that it changed the colour of the queen's eyes from black to blue.

The Shadow land is a land inhabited by spirits and the inhabitants call it the land of truth, where things are revealed. They stood staring at each other; billows of cloud from the heavens descended down and obscured their view and, the dragon was-swallowed in it taken by the spirits to its own home; somewhere in the Shadow land. While there, he brought his magical mirror, whooshed his breath on to the mirror, transformed it to a screening material, and sat on its leg observing the queen and the librarian. They were so

18

confused, lost in the emptiness of the land where everyone was invisible-barely a sense of feeling could predict if someone was around. They began wandering to where their thoughts led them, which in fact turned out to be nowhere. The queen went ahead of the librarian and stoop hitting her sword on the ground. Suddenly, mandrakes quickly shot up lifting her higher as they grew to large trees. An old woman appeared to them looking so cranky and scary with her face dotted with elephant pimples, sores that were very rare. Below was something different, the flesh on her legs was rotten and chunks of it fell as she was approached the queen. Her odour was just too strong, that it made the queen very nauseous, Armand stood, watching her every step. She walked and stood before the powerful mandrake plant and commanded the plant to release the queen to her. The leaves of the plant merged with each other forming a slippery platform from which the queen slid down and touched her leg down just before the old witch.

'Give me your hands' said the old witch. The queen gazed at her for a while and turned and looked at Armand, then pulled her sword from its case and pointed at the old witch and asked,

'Who are you?

'I'm the seer and witch of this great Shadow land, the true future and present of the spirits of this land' said the old witch.

'Prove it' said the queen.

The old witch stared at her for a while and did nothing. The queen continued,

'I know you' said the queen

'You know me? Asked the old witch, the queen stood sighing.

'How well? She continued

'You are just one of the *tantans* to derail and rip me off my quest to saving my land but let me tell you, I have been warned by the great dragon that nothing here is real.'

'The dragon?! Said the old witch

'Yes! One of the most powerful magician that ever lived, he wrote the book of chantals to help us save our land,' said the queen

'The dragon?! Is that what he told you,' said the old witch 'hahahaha' giggled the old witch.

The old witch turned behind her and harvested cocoyam leaves placed them on the ground, then, sat on it and said to her;

'Sit down my daughter.'

She sat and Armand walked closer to them and sat beside them ignoring the odour from the old woman.

'My daughter, I have lived for more than seven thousand years and I have seen things you cannot possibly imagine both those that existed in the past and those yet to come. My name is Sistercianata and I am a great witch of this land. The dragon was never a magician but the true god of war,' said Sistercianata

'What?!

'Yes!' Replied Sistercianata

The queen exclaimed turned and looked at Armand, he was even more surprised.

'Duce was cursed by the gods because a powerful sorcerer lived there and engaged the gods into battle. When he was defeated, the gods cursed the land. After hundreds of years, humans from neighbouring kingdoms who were the outlaws of that kingdom, migrated to Duce and occupied the land. The gods wanted to destroy them. The dragon - the god of war who captured the evil sorcerer had to plead with the gods to show mercy on the inhabitants of the land. Krurice, the god of dead disguised himself as the god of war and went to Duce and deceived the inhabitants-enchanting spells and causing wars amongst nations standing on your side meanwhile he had his other angels as god in the other kingdoms doing just the same like him. He was intelligent and knew what he was doing, his army are the army of dead and he keeps on killing the living to increase his army to one-day wage war on the living increasing his dominion to be able to challenge the gods. He was doing this because he was exiled from the planet of the gods. His aim has been to hurt the gods, the gods were not blind, they had their ways of doing things and wanted to capture him alive and imprison him in their most secret chamber where he would have lived forever.

'He was using the king your father and when he realised it, he turned against him. The woes of Duce unfolded and your cries reached the ears of Zalinda another great wizard who came to rescue you all. He thought he was doing the right thing engaging the god of dead in a war but he was wrong and realised it after he had killed the god of dead-krurice whom the gods had wanted alive. He had to pay with his life to appease the gods and returned to his kingdom. A few years later, you all turned away from the gods and they were angry and had to banish the god of war from the planet of the dragons because he was the one who had pleaded with the gods to let you be and they saw it as mockery for the insult you all blasted on them. They turned their backs on you all and Krurice in the underworld now used the opportunity to send his deadly creatures to the land to win more souls to his kingdom to fulfil his plans on waging a war with the living. Because the gods are still angry at your kingdom, you needed to embark on this quest so that Zalinda can help cleanse you and your land by performing a ritual to appease the gods. Indeed, the dragon wrote the book of Chantal but as a precaution.' Said the old witch

'Why does the dragon not...?' asked the queen

'Wait' the witch interrupted,'

She listened to the echo of the air for a while and said,

'You must go now,' she said and gave them a staff and told them that the staff will help them when need arises. Armand turned round and round searching for her to no avail. He then got back to the queen curiously,

'Where is the old witch?' he asked

'You saw it yourself, she's gone to the temple of witches' said the queen

At once, the mandrake started shrinking, sunk itself to the ground and vanished. The queen quickly rushed to it, cut off one of its leaves and roots, and gave it to Armand to put in his sack and they started walking ahead into the Secret land of Ascador - the place of deadly magic. In this land, virtue is a sin, good is a crime and love is a taboo with trust being a sacrilege and everything in this land was angry to be disturbed. Their enchantments are very powerful and they are perfect in performing the black magic of ancient times. No creature has ever gone into this land and lived to tell the story. Even the gods are afraid of this land. Krurice plan was to go into the land and convince the creatures in there to be his allies so that, they can wage a war against the living and the dead. At the gate, upon entering the land of Ascador, Krurice had positioned his army so that no one can gain access into the land except him. He knew if he had them by his side, the gods would be doomed. The land of the living would be in dead chaos having no one for support. Creatures of this land are called the Efuans. However, despite their ways, they have a leader and laws, which govern them. Armand was the one who first noticed the army of the dead whom the old witch had made mentioned of, and signalled the queen.

'Look,' he pointed and the queen saw for herself the legion of this army headed by Krurice that had surrounded the gate of Ascador. The queen raised her head and saw them, and, reached out for her sword. Then, she ran close to a guava tree and hid behind it, spying on what the army and Krurice were doing-they were marching forward and backward in a regular pattern.

Back at the shadow land; the dragon had seen everything in his screening mirror, and took a deep breath in fear of what might happen to them if they ventured into the territory of the army of dead without intelligence. He rose and stood on all fours still gazing at the mirror and the content he had screed.

Chapter 3

Krurice adjusted himself three times, and, knocked the gate of Ascador. The guards of Ascador opened the gate, seized him and questioned him,

'Who are you and what's your mission in the land of Ascador?' said the Efuan guard

'I'm Krurice, the god of the dead,' he replied with confidence.

'God of the dead?!' They asked, baffled; releasing him. He adjusted himself again and again and said to them,

'I demand to see your leader, Lord Fontematier Gurugazi.'

The four guards who had held him hostage, bowed before him and said to him;

'He's at the Prime place in Melrose; we'll consult with him first before getting back to you.'

He gave a forward nod of his head and one of the Efuan guards ran to Melrose and told Lord Fontematier. He stood up from his seat and wondered;

'Why is the god of the dead in my land?' he thought for a while searching and scanning through his mind for old memories and possible answers, it took a while for his vain search and he turned and asked the guard.

'Did he disclose his mission?' asked Fontematier

'No, he was just determined to see you,' the guard replied.

Fontematier turned and feeling the bane atmosphere and said to the guards,

'Bring him before me.'

The two guards rushed back to the gate and led Krurice to the premises of their lord. When they met, their eyes clashed, their hearts beat faster and series of enchantments ran through their mouths to calm the powers of each other, making themselves normal again. A red flash burst out in and made a boundary between the two men. Then, their powers laid to rest, they both frowned. At once, the Lord asked him,

'What's your mission in the land of Ascador?'

'For alliance, Lord Fontematier,' said Krurice

'The Efuans make no friends and make no enemies; they are independent....' The Lord replied

'We all know the truth here, you were once the gods and lived in the planet of the gods, but you defiled the gods' code and slept with humans and the gods cursed you and transformed your head into that of a snake, making your hands have scales and your legs covered with fur. They reduced your toes to three, rejected you, and exiled you from their planet. You found refuge here in Ascador. Before you left, you stole something from the gods; their powers embedded in the powerful book of *Cranile*. Year after year, you have studied the enchantment and have become very powerful that even the gods are now scared of you. They are looking for all means to destroy this land and you all. What you do not know is that, humans conceived and bore of your fruit, for two thousand years, they have been modified and looked like humans. One of them was in Duce kingdom, he did not know the powers he possessed, and the king killed him because of me. The gods became furious and cursed the land the more; they actually wanted to use him to attack this land because they knew you share the same bond of love that people of the same kind do. He is now with me and I have made him discovered his powers. I am here, - the gods want to destroy you, which of course I know you would not let that happen - I want to destroy the gods and the land of the living and subject them to my control. We need this alliance for our mutual benefit,' said Krurice.

Lord Fontematier turned and gazed at the empty space, sighed, then turned and said to him,

'Sit' He pointed a seat for him to sit on. The spirits gave way and he walked and sat on the seat offered to him by Fontematier. In effect, he had agreed to his friendship and saw reasons for it.

A few minutes later, a blue flame sparkled and lit the whole area, they both rose from their seats. The army of the dead quickly searched the areas outside to find the cause of the fire; the guards went out of the gate searching too. Actually, the queen had enchanted a spell, which ignited the fire; she quickly jumped in a nearby bush and hid. The army of dead and the Efuans intensified their search and captured Armand. He tried to enchant his magical word to escape from them to no avail; they had used their powers to numb his magic. The queen watched him been dragged on the ground to the land of Ascador. She covered her mouth with her hand and remained silent. The Efuan guards dragged Armand and took him before Lord Fontematier and Krurice,

'Take him to Isler,' said Lord Fontematier. Isler is a place where captured intruders are tortured and even killed. They took him there and hung him on a rope, clothed him in a dress made of thorns and pushed him on one side allowing him to be swinging from one end to another colliding with a wall they had built at each end. The thorns pierced his body and blood oozed out freely. He cried aloud but no one was there to help. The Efuans and Krurice stood laughing. They wanted to gain information from him and that never happened so they kept on tormenting him.

Outside the gates of Ascador, the queen was confused with no idea as to where she would go. Then she remembered the staff of clehem that was in Armand's bag, which had fallen at one corner of the bush during the time of his capture. She went and looked for it and removed the staff and took it with her matching away from the gate of Ascador. She walked for a distance of four miles and sat on a large rock along the road resting. Seven divine spirits visited her, she was scared, it was like the Halloween; she pulled out her sword quickly enchanting within her heart preparing herself to engage the spirit in combat. They had perceived it and shouted at her to stop. She raised her head up and looked at them and they looked at her. Without wasting time, the spirits joined their hands pushing it forward, whooshes their mana into her body and transforming her into one of the Efuans and said to her;

'Go queen of Duce and rescue Armand, we have now realised that your mission becomes our mission. You have thirty minutes to save him and get out of the land after which you would then be-retransformed into your normal self. Delay may be dangerous.' They disappeared.

The queen placed the staff of clehem in a safe place inside her armour and set on a quick run to the land of Ascador. As she was running, she became under attack by the spirits of the shadow land who saw her as enemy, she stopped to fight them and her time was running out. When she succeeded in defeating them, she rested for a minute then set on a run to the land of Ascador. She finally arrived and the gatekeepers opened the gate for her. She got in and looked about scanning them all trying to figure out where Armand could have been send. Josephine was unable to figure out; she called one of the Efuans and asked,

'Where has the newly captured enemy been taken to?' she asked looking straight into his eyes.

'Have you been sleeping, are you sure you have been in this land? If you were, then you should have known that he has been taken to the temple. Tomorrow, he will be thrown into the pot of *Wenesance*.' Said the *Efuan*s

The pot of *wenesance* sound strange to her, she had never heard of it before and knew nothing about it, she looked at him deep into his eyes then backed out and was scared to ask too many questions especially about the pot which he made mention of arousing suspicions. She went and sat next to another Efuan and engaged her in a conversation,

'I can't imagine how his body would look like when he is finally dipped in to the pot of *Wenesance*,' said Josephine gazing at her with fear of what she might say next.

'Oh yes,' she replied, 'his body will dissolved and his blood drank by all bringing strength and powers to us,' she said smiling.

The queen quickly understood the use of the pot, left her, and went to the area where they hung him. The pot of *wenesance* is a large pot full of concoctions and magical substances. The Efuans usually used the pot for rituals. When intruders are thrown in, their bodies melt and they drink of it together with their blood. To them, it gives them more powers as they are able to absorb their *mana* and add to theirs. It is usually their best day.

Immediately, the queen removed his sword, killed four of the guards guarding the area where Armand was, and stormed in. When Armand saw her, she appeared to him as the queen and he was happy, and she shut him up by placing her finger on his lips. Then, she untied the chains and thorns worn on him and took him out of the place. She went with him under the roots of a large umbrella tree. He was very weak; she removed a cloth from her bag and a bottle of water, poured water on the cloth and used it to clean his wounds then bandaged them and laid him to rest while she stood watching. She has only fifteen more minutes to vacate the place before she retransforms into her normal self. It was now difficult for her to take Armand out because he was in his normal form and wanted by the Efuans. Her magic was too weak to transform Armand into an Efuan and walk him out. She stood confused and calculating. Time was running out fast, the Efuans had now discovered the four dead guards and knew there were traitors in their midst. They were ransacking everywhere. The two leaders were very furious and placed their armies at the gate for no one to go out or come in. The queen reached out to her sword, cut off tree branches and grasses and covered Armand with it. She then rushed to meet the rest of the Efuans; they were so restless moving about still searching for their prey. One of the Efuans came closer to the pile of branches and stood closer to it. Armand woke up and shook and the branches got displaced. The Efuans used his spear and scattered the branches and saw Armand, he was about to scream. The queen came from behind and pierced him with her sword; closing his mouth and watched him died quietly.

'What happened, who are you?' asked Armand, this time, she appeared as one of the Efuans.

'Shh! I'm your queen in disguise,' the queen silencing him, placing her finger on his lips. She supported him and stood him up. He stood up still weak and unstable. She taps him, and asked,

'What do we do next?'

Armand gazed at her and asked;

'Where is the staff?'

She removed it from somewhere inside her body, under her armour and gave it to him. He took it, smiled and said,

'I thought we had lost it'

The queen stood watching him with curiosity and waiting for him to come up with an idea on how they should escape from the land of Ascador, no idea was forth coming from him. She got angry and pierced her sword on the ground, biting her fingers. She had only four minutes for her body to return to normal. She was confused and frustrated. She tried using her magic to transform Armand again to no avail. After moving up and about without any ideas, her minutes finally elapsed; her body became intensely cold and she started shivering violently. Her eyes turned red and her body appeared to be stiff, her veins were all tensed, at once; she started cackling. After one minute of being in this state, her mouth opened and a strange spirit came out of her mouth in the form of soot and disappeared in to the air and she came back to normal. The queen bent her head down and raised it up and turned to look at Armand but saw the army of dead and Efuans who had surrounded them. Her cackles had led them to the where she was. She pulled out her sword to fight, Krurice stretched forth his hand and whooshed a *mana*, which turned her sword into ashes, and the particles flew into the atmosphere and settled on their heads. Krurice turned and looked at Fontematier and smiled. Fontematier walked to her, seized her from her hair and asked,

'Who are you?'

The queen looked at him and uttered no word. Krurice came from behind and said to him.

'The daughter of the former king who killed one of your own'

'Is she dead, how come she is in the spirit world?' asked Fontematier.

'She has been fortified and on the quest to saving her land from the cursed of the gods,' Said Krurice.

Fontematier allowed her hair and told the guards to lock them up; they seized them both and locked them up.

The dragon had seen everything in his temple using his screening mirror, he took a deep breath, and conjured a powerful necklace, which was dark gold in colour with a ruin of *sundicel* on it-an ancient magic that was able to summon the gods and Zalinda by anyone who possessed it. He then enchanted and called on a pigeon, placed the necklace on its neck and put powerful but small gneiss on its mouth then enchanted a spell again sending the birds to Josephine.

The bird took the necklace and the gneiss to her, wore it on her neck, and put the stone in her mouth then left. The necklace burned red and the queen's eyes changes to blue, she enchanted a powerful word of magic; which cast a spell and it break the chains used in chaining Armand and freed him. He in turn went to the queen and untied her too.

Without wasting time, the queen immediately invoked the seven divine spirits who helped her into getting into the land of Ascador, and they appeared before her. Each of them wearing a white garment, with fine black hair long enough to rest on their hips. Seven minutes later, the great gods from the planet of the gods appeared; stood looking at them without uttering any word. The seven divine spirits went closer to the great god and bowed before him. Josephine and Armand bowed too but the god stood static still without any action or uttering any word thus.

The dragon immediately sensed it, he enchanted a powerful magic, and the powers, took from the queen the staff of clehem and dropped it on the table of Zalinda. He was sitting on his relaxed chair resting; suddenly he noticed the staff. He stretched his hand to pick the staff, an infrared light flashed from nowhere and encrypted on the staff in an ancient writing; fueah quitta ohgo, fueah quitta ohgo neah nah ngoeh' meaning, come and help your mother, come and help your mother in the farm of trouble. He picked it up and looked closely at the staff. He quickly understood where the staff was from and knew its purpose.

He went and performed sophisticated ritual burning incense and murmuring incantations and enchantments- begging the gods to have mercy upon the children of Duce and on the land. When he had finished, he went into his temple and dressed in his garment. A streak of love emotions went in a form of a powerful wind to the great god; he sniffed it like the find fragrances of a perfume. His heart opened up, and the mantle of darkness that had painted his heart obscuring the plea and struggles of the people of Duce was cleansed immediately- mercy and love bathed his heart. The contempt at which he had been seeing the people of Duce disappears. He looked at the queen and said to her.

'My daughter, fear no more, I have come, I have come,' said the great god.

It was the D-day and, the Efuans were about to use the queen and Armand for their rituals. The lord had sent seven of the Efuan guards to bring the queen and Armand before him. They opened the door and the great god would not even let their unclean presents mingled with his. He clapped his hands and a powerful spell spread in powerful turbulences and pushed them away. They hit the ground, six died on the spot and the last one ran off and informed the lord. A few seconds later, all the rivers, lakes and streams in the whole of Ascador began boiling and bubbles rose. The escaped guard had not reached Fontematier yet but he had felt the powers of a strange force in his land; His chair in which he sat had disappeared. The guard arrived,

'My lord,' said the guard.

'Inform my commander to see me now,' said Fontematier. The guard was surprised why he did not want to listen to him especially with the important message he had to covey to him. He ran and informed the commander as the lord had said but what he did not know was that, Fontematier had understood everything going on. He never wanted him to speak out to him and have the opportunity of passing on the message to the rest of them instilling tension. According to their law, should anything happen in the land whether good or bad, the people present at the scene must inform the lord before daring to whisper it to any other person. He knew by preventing him from not conveying the message, he would tell no one about the cause of the death of their brothers and they would not know that the great god was in their land for revenge causing panic. He wanted to tell them himself by quickly rallying them to perform a ritual-to muster their strength, boost their magic and calm their adrenaline before telling them whom they were to meet in battle. The commander heard his message, and ran to him.

'Summon all the Efuans' said Fontematier. He did, and the ritual was performed, and, he told them who they were to engage in battle. It was a shock to them because they were all surprised at the sudden appearance of the great god. They knew that before his coming to their land to attack and collect the great magic book of cranile, three sign were to be visible; the stars were to blink three times, the tree roots that clutches the ground were to be loosen and their leaves all shed, all the waters were to dry off. They have read all these and it did not happened the way they had expected-still they had no choice other than saving their land and the Efuans in it.

Krurice summoned all the Splimiide in the land of the living to the land of Ascador, to fight for him. They came in their numbers, he commanded them to search through the land of Ascador and attack the great god. At the same time, Zalinda had prepared himself and disappeared from the

Gravel land and appeared in the land of Ascador. He bowed before the great god and the seven divine spirits.

A few seconds later, all the Efuans, the Splimiide and the army of dead together with their leaders raided the area where they were; powers met powers, enchantments met enchantments and magic against magic. They fought and fought and after five hours of fighting, the great god cast a spell - a powerful hurricane passed over the land and swept everything killing the Efuans and the army of dead. He went and collected the great magic book. Krurice was bleeding. He captured him and caged him in a magic cage. At once, Zalinda took the staff of Clehem, struck the ground with it and cried out loudly, the sand swept away from where they stood to the east, north, south and west. Thunder struck and the air seemed to be in violent motion. Darkness and light engaged in a bloody battle. The earth appeared to be contracting and expanding. Finally, light conquered and its rays reflected in the vent of the chamber directly to the queen's eyes, she opened her eyes and squinted and realised it was a dream. The queen woke up with her body aching and stiff. She let out a grand, lazy yawn and stretched her stiff limbs. Before she can complete her stretch, she catches a glimpse of the long nails at the end of her fingers and then the long hair that had covered her body. Alarmed, she rushed to the mirror and frantically removed the thick layer of dust covering it. She looked at herself in the mirror and let out a terrifying scream. She has aged. She realized she has been sleeping for 40 years. Her scream awakes her servants. They jump out of their beds and dutifully rush to their queen's aid but their legs are stiff and their voices croak as they call each other. From her screams and the servants' voices -carried from part of the palace to the other - the entire village is also woken up. Suddenly there is pandemonium everywhere; in between shrieks and confusion, everybody stares at each other with disbelief. Some are found dead; pregnant women had died along with their unborn babies and the elderly were no more. They all realize that they have aged and look scrawny having slept for 40 years.

Josephine had to act fast. She called the few elders who had not died to assess the situation and to find ways of dealing with the matter of procreation. Most women had reached menopause and the men had become too old and weak to start families. Tears ran down her cheek.

'How far have the mighty fallen? Our enemies will now become the genealogy of our nation,' Said the queen.

.

Chapter 4

The old age

After three years, a young lad went up to one of the elders and asked him to tell him the story of the land of Duce. He gazed the emptiness and pool of tears filled his eyes just waiting for a blink to run down his cheek, he looked at him then rested comfortably on his chair and started;

"It was a forgettable age; when the moon's mooning was important and the candle's flame was as useful as the electricity of modern age. The contempt of human despair and the glowering that went across the horizon, the work of magic and human creativities weaved in the kingdom of darkness- an ancient kingdom where virgins were used for sacrifices to the gods and hopes barely uncertain, in a land far, far away. Their cradles twitched for kingdom sake and the forest seemed lonely in the brightness of the day because even the animals were afraid of the laws of the land; they escaped into their habitats and only went out at night to communicate with their comrade. Yet again, another king was to rule the kingdom of Duce. The crowd, the people of the Duce Kingdom gathered and cheered at him just after his inauguration on the throne. They hoped his enthronement would be a new era for the people of Duce. His father had been a nightmare in the land of Duce; freedom was what they sought. Would the new king walk against the path of his father or follow in his footsteps? That was what the people of Duce were yet to discover, but from his eyes, he looked so humble and gentle- the face that every child, every woman and every man in the land of Duce would love to see on the throne. Judging him from his looks would yield no fruit and so they stayed patiently to see his policies as the newly crowned king of Duce kingdom. Would he stop the sacrifice of humans to gods and end the beheadings of criminals in the land or would he continue just like his father? They wondered and were so eager to know, because if he did; then the land would remain in chaos.

The king knew and was not afraid to die but he was troubled that the gods may attempt to fight leaving the land with carnages of the people he hope to sacrifice.

An hour later, the king was due to present himself before his people, dressed in his ceremonial garment-crossed with ranks of his title and a beautifully coloured ivory staff he held in his right hand; an ancestral symbol of power. The king's guard opened the chamber door and the king walked, and stood at the balcony on the fourth floor of his facade castle and waved his closed palms that held the ivory staff tightly to his people, and they raised their heads up, clapped for the king, and shouted in excitement.

'Long live the king, long live the king'

After he had finished addressing his people, he turned and walked back into his chamber.

What he said was catastrophic; and, their stomachs began churning with anger and the smiles of the people of Duce became sour, the errant breeze from the south end passed over and swept their voices to the wilderness and only the noise of rustling tree leaves could be heard yet they kept on smiling.

The target was about the laws of the land, which were the same. He was even worse than his father, they reckoned and, the thought sprouted in the minds of the people to yank off the crown from his head immediately before he could do worse than his father. However, no one dared to say this to the neighbour, lest they be charged with treason. They feared the power of the throne and the curse involved in tradition and, sank their grudges to move on. Who were you to challenge the king, mere commoner? For forty years, they have known no peace ever since they had a king, and have lived like slaves in their own fatherland and for forty years blood has been shed in the land of Duce. Who was now the enemy, the king or their neighbours with whom they warred all the time? The answer to their questions remained buried in their minds. The king had no mercy and defaulters to the laws of the land were beheaded- they were given no chance to stay in prison or to serve a visible punishment.

'When we are surrounded by enemies, what do we do, do we save our kingdom or let it loose? It would have been better if the enemies where only humans- even the gods had decided to war against us in alliance with our enemies and crushed and ruined our kingdom. We knew not our future and, our fatherland became strange to our eyes because of the crude and harsh conditions we were subjected to. Suppressing our enemies below our heels are our priorities,' were the reasons for their tight laws and the thoughts the king went to and rose from the bed with. This was true and exactly what the kingdom of Duce solely wants-and the zeal in triumphing and keeping the kingdom stake and head of the other kingdoms saw them in alliance with magic too. Nevertheless, nothing comes without a price and some had to sacrifice for others to benefit.

Chapter 5

The people of Duce had a life different from those of the entire world and they still live by it. The king was the final judge and no matter how angry they were concerning the law, they tried as much to keep it within them and embrace their laws with scrutiny. They feared their king and trusted in his judgement. In the land of Duce, only the king was allowed to marry more than one wife. When the king saw a woman and loved her, he ordered his men to put a bracelet around her ankles. After seven days, she would be invited to the palace and the elders would perform some traditional rites; a piece of enchantment, blessed water from a bowl thrown on the floor drop wise to bless the couple and a traditional handing of the crown to her before the people. Every other person in the land was entitled to only one wife; you have to divorce the previous wife before marrying a new one. The new wife should not be a virgin but a divorcee. Their women never had sex before marriage and knew nothing about it until in their married homes except those who were divorced, that was their law.

Before marriage, the elders of the land would gather with the bridegroom in the bride's house with goats and sheep to offer to the bride's parent and family together with gallons of traditional wine to show them appreciation for grooming their daughter ripe for marriage. Then the elders would spread a thin white sheet on an empty mattress to cover it. They would dance round and round about it drinking their own wine separate from that given to the parent of the bride, spitting some in the air, hitting their staff and clapping their hands, crooning with bases to vibrate their current environ. The bride would walk pass in their middle and stand on the mattress and undress, and then lie flat on the mattress with her stomach upward facing the heavens. Another elder would blow his flute; the bridegroom would walk just like the bride had done on to the mattress and undress. The elders would raise their tone, singing and clapping their hands and the bridegroom would penetrate the bride. When blood flows from the bride's break-up on to the sheet, they would hey and cheered at the couple giving their blessings. That was how they got married. If no blood flew, then, the bride is immediately reported to the king and, they would know she lost her virginity before marriage, which meant, she had betrayed the land by fornicating. The king would instruct his most powerful commander, Shaakhan- who would behead the woman and her head held above his height would drop into a burning furnace, beside the shrine, in front of Duce people and their king.

Shaakhan was a highly skilled, brave, seven-foot warrior of Duce in charge of any beheadings in the land. He also commanded the king's warriors to war, he was the king best warrior and his right hand man in he confided some matters of the kingdom. Anytime he went into a home, the neighbours would peep to see who was next to be beheaded. They never thought for once that matters of the heart could take him to any home because, he was seen only occasionally and he hardly smiled, only once when you come to think of it, when the king was about to welcome another bride in his palace.

The king was bent on crushing all his enemies, he asked Shaakhan to gather all his warriors before him. He did, he gathered five million warriors under his command in the land of Duce before the king's presence. He saw them, smiled, and summoned Krurice- the god of war to bless his warriors before they embarked on the frontline with their enemies. A heavy breeze blew past spinning in circles and from it, Krurice appeared before the people and his eyes burned green. A virgin's head was cut off and the blood spilled around in a circle where Krurice stood, he raised his hand and blessed the swords, spears and arrows of the warriors, the warriors felt the power and bowed before Krurice and the king. The king raised his hands, stretched it to the front and blessed the warriors, punching the air several times to instil courage and strength in to their hearts,

'For the kingdom,' the king said.

'For the kingdom, for our king huaaaaa,' the warriors replied roaring and raising their sword, arrows and spears right up in the air and Shaakhan led them to battle with their enemies.

At the battle field, Shaakhan lined up his warriors in half-moon patterns, placing his reserves and back-up warriors at the wings and butt of the pattern, stood before them and roared,

'Fighting for the kingdom'

And the rest of the warriors roared suit,

'Fighting for the kingdom, in the name of our king and our god Krurice, huaaaaaaaaa,' their voices could be heard right deep at the very heart of their enemy's kingdom, and he would give them instruction,

'Attack'

Raising his shield fitted in his hand just above his chest and his right hand holding his spear far above his head pushing forward his hand to the direction of the enemy for his warriors to attack. His height was reasonable and every warrior could see him at the same time. The warriors attacked with a speed above a hundred miles per hour, holding firmly in their hands their shields with their swords, attacking and slaying their enemies one after the other. They were tireless and fought fearlessly taking on their enemies right deep into their camps, no end at the battlefield was better. As their swords clashed, the land ran red and they circled and crushed them both on the plane and in their furrows, dipping and yanking out their swords and spears they had pierced into the chest and through the heart of their enemies, they stumbled to the ground. When the enemy saw their strength, they were baffled and retreated. The warriors of Duce followed them in to their own kingdom demanding the head of their king and nothing could stop them with the force with which they rushed into the palaces of their enemies, the Brook Kingdom, which was one of their fierce enemies. When the king saw that there was no way for him and his warriors to continue to defend the Brooks, he caught a white cock and brought before the commander of Duce warrior. It meant peace and surrendering in the arms of the warriors of the Duce to be their slaves. However, the commander was under instruction from their king to bring the head of the King of the Brooks to his palace so that he could use it to decorate the shrine of the god of war, Krurice. Two of his warriors held the Brook's king arm to arm, turning his face to be darting at the sea of blood from the warriors slays in battle; with blood crusting down their bodies, and, they brought him before Shaakhan. He first gave him a bitter look then turns around as if he had forgotten that he existed, gazing at his warrior, panting and vibrating to slaughter more warriors of the Brook's kingdom, jumping and shaking their bodies ready to take command from their commander, the king of the Brook spoke,

'I demand to see your king to...'

Shaakhan would not let the authoritative word from his mouth slide through and disturb the quiet air, seized the sword of one of his warriors and stroke through the king's neck and his head fell off and bounced three times on the ground. The warriors of Duce raised their sword to the heavens and 'hey' the name of their king and their god. A messenger went quickly and informed their king and he prepared his horses and chariots to meet his warriors at the boarder upon entering the kingdom. Shaakhan instructed one of his warriors to pick up the Brook king's head and put into his bag and he did, and they took it to their king. The king was very happy, he had instructed the women of Duce to prepare food for the warriors and when they arrived, they danced and ate and drank the best wine from the best wine tapper in the kingdom and got drunk and slept on their swords till the morning was nigh. That was the first bloody and heroic battle of Duce and anyone in the kingdom could notice the smiles of the king's commander in his flamboyant warriors dress.

The king was very pleased with Shaakhan and gave him his only daughter for marriage. The king's daughter loved neither her father nor Shaakhan because of their crude brutality to the people of Duce but she was the king's daughter and had to play by the rules of royalty and avoid being killed by his father or Shaakhan the killer of the kingdom. Playing by the rules meant adhering and following the path of tradition and Josephine, the king's daughter had no choice. All she wished was the day the kingdom's power would change hands into someone who cares and stopped the wicked and crude way of treating their sick and disabled in the land of Duce. Every passing day, one human or animal was beheaded in the kingdom of Duce, and their pain would touch down at the marrow of Josephine and she would lament in plaintive secretly on their behalf. She was the nicest woman with power in the kingdom to save them but with her father in authority, she could hardly think straight, whimpering as she watched them being killed.

The king, her father, believed in magic, spells of their ancestors and strength of his warriors. However, he did not believe in nature's warrant that flew through the land and arrested his people randomly. That nature's warrant was sickness and he called those affected by it weak people. He knew the gods were protecting their land and they made annual sacrifices to them, so, there was no reason why the gods would allow curses to foul their land. The sick were the criminals, those who had sex before marriage, had abortions and committed treason. All these crimes had a greater punishment and the individual losing his or her head before the people by the royal sword that always glinted before the cut- the indigenes would shout, 'oooooo,' in chorus, howling and turning their faces on one side, clutching each other- twisting their mouth and watching blood oozing and spilling down the fathoms. He would gaze at them for a while then raise his eyes up to still their noise then look at them again for a while. 'This will serve as a lesson to all those who hope to betray the law, in doing so they've betrayed me and the land,' said the king and would walk back into his chamber silently and they would be left whimpering in desperation, cursing the king in their minds for the evil and pain he's causing the people.

When the princess's fertile period was nearer, she would deny sleeping with Shaakhan until it elapsed then she would return in bed with him again replenishing lost romances and cuddles feeling themselves to the fullest and the past frays would quickly be forgotten. She did so because she did not want her child's father to be a murderer; she understood if he killed someone in battle but not slaying the innocent because of their sickness. She wanted him to be a man to oppose the king- make him know killing the criminals was not the best way to punish the individual, however, doing that would seemed like committing suicide. The thought to see the people lament for their love ones was troublesome,

'These are common crimes that the kingdom deemed unforgivable,' she thought.

They were very passionate about themselves and no murder was ever reported in the land except those in battles or those killed by the royal sword or sacrificed to the gods. Their king had a sensible way of forcing them wave their grief. Every household whose members had been killed by the royal sword was chosen at random, to work in the royal palace and earn the benefits for working there. This raised their standards and pride. To some families, it excited them and they forgot their pain easily while others went along with it but never let their emotions shoot out. The king's determination made him very strong and he captured all the four kingdoms that usually posed a threat to the Duce kingdom in the time of his father and made them his slaves, and they worked in their plantations and in other areas of duties paying huge taxes to the king.

Two years after Josephine's marriage to Shaakhan, they were still without a child and she never wanted the people to question her ability to conceive-raising alarm that would echo in the kings ears, taking her to another dark-side of tradition; the shaving of her hair and the marriage to another woman by Shaakhan. She had begun nursing plans to sneak into one of the four kingdoms and get herself pregnant before returning to her homeland and make Shaakhan to bear the responsibility. She hated her father but it was obvious-like people say, "you shouldn't bite the fingers that feed you," the same was true for her. She needed her father more than anything and she struggled to restrain herself from things that would cause her to be banished from the kingdom or possibly beheaded, knowing that she was next to the throne-saw her.

Her mother died in hunting, eaten by a wild and hungry lion with her servant in the thick and lonely forest east of Duce was the message that echoed in the Indigenes' ears. In fact, she had challenged the king and he killed her and buried her somewhere no one could trace and cooked up this story and told them. They believed him especially with the evidence he had shown them. Marrying the princess was a gift to Shaakhan and by law, he would be the traditional prime minister and he would rule one of the captured kingdoms, possibly the Brook kingdom answerable to the king of Duce.

Every six months, the indigenes usually gathered at the city squares to confess their sins to the elders of their various cities and they in turn gave them advice on how to get along. However, matters concerning rape, loss of virginity and sickness were reported to the king. When confessing, they avoided mentioning unlawful deeds so as not to implicate themselves though in some cases, their friends or family betrayed them because they wanted a reward from the king. The king's harshness to the weak made most of the people to be very secretive and they feared to communicate sensitive matters, not even with their children. In some cases, before they could do so, it meant they trusted you with all their hearts and were sure you would not betray them and have their head chop off by the king. It was true, no matter how hard or strict their king was, things still went unnoticed in the kingdom and the king was baffled when he heard them. A young man wrote to the council of elders of the village confessing to them what had been happening in his family. He wrote;

'My name is Michael Leed, the lone son of my parents as I knew. By the time you finish reading these words, I would be gone to Wonderland, which is where I am from. Only the loving smiles of your pore to these compassionate and affectionate words of mine would nestle the courage deep within me to be able to face the king in judgement. I know it was not my fault but every human has its own destiny and as opposed to weather, it is far from predictable, waking up every morning in the shadows of my dreams to a destiny far from home. I had to give it up and succumb to what life had to offer me, like a child, we are all written in the world of hope and believes, the fortresses of life unknown and yet its path it's paved for us. How was I to know? Nevertheless, things turned around for me and I was around to sedate its wildness. The gentleness of my whole was able to resist my frustration and I smacked my mistake with no pity. This was how it all started.

Rose Green had been whispering gently; forcing her tongue to scratch all the angles of her palates and releasing coordinated sounds from her thoughts, causing her to gulp repeatedly as she swallowed her saliva. She had ambitions and I wished it had gone as planned. Everything that sprang into her mind was something, something more critical, radical and sensational. Leaving her lonely in her room thinking and speaking aloud without her noticing.

'The world's beautiful and the creativeness of humanity makes it even more amazing. What will I give to the person I will spend the rest of my life with? I know I am a teenager, I am only sixteen. But how do I plan for an even more promising life that would not only restore my pride as a woman but will make me excessively very precious in the eyes of the beholder? Maybe flowers could even be more beautiful or the gift of human creativities! Hmmmm! I am confused here and I don't know what to do because all these are vast and common. I have read scrolls about broken marriages and I have read about couples' mistrust to one another and, I've seen before my own eyes at the village square the cruelty of some couples killing an entire family, maybe because of a certain misconstrue or perhaps a lurid event that could have aggravated the scene.' She thought looking in bareness, paused for a while and continued.

'I would want to stop incidents like this from happening to my relationship and make a difference, changing my world from a world of catapulting vicissitude of human kind, a dynamism of sadistic characters in to a more promising and disciplinary aspect of life. I know that sometimes men could be so cruel and opportunistic.' She thought, saying it loudly without noticing how loud she was because she was consumed by the sweetness of her thinking. A flying mosquito landed on her leg, and started sucking her. She slapped the area with great force killing the mosquito. She then placed her hand on her chest and continued to think.

'I'm scared of venturing into a withering mistake keeping in mind the realities of life. Sometimes, I feel some couples fall out because of the lack of discipline to adapt, to compromise from the principles of their spouses, which in some cases have led to anger and a horrible and unexpected behaviour. Some of this horrible behaviour sometimes goes unharmed. The mystery of avoiding these vices are my wonderland and the preamble of my selection to whomever I would share the rest of my life, I damn the king's madness of the law because no man will stand at my door to ask for my hand in marriage and I accept without me loving him. This is absurd to my friends who on many occasions have told me that, it could lead to me not getting married at the end, which of course I would rather not than enslaving myself to someone I'll barely know.' She sighed and continued

'I know the truth, my sister was swept from the emotions of love and fell in the arms of the wrong person who ill-treated her and she ended up in an awkward position in my father's house. I have to be careful and look in to the eyes of the person who will claim to love me and see if he's worth it!' She thought, leaning backwards on her armchair and gazing intensely at the ceiling.

That was her way of thinking and like every woman, she will want to meet a gentle and loving person to have fun with and get familiar with him before possibly getting married. Her thoughts were not different from mine-and I fed my every day loneliness with the generation fantasy, I'd have done the same and if I was in her shoes, I would not only be careful but extremely very careful and vigilant. Like they say, meeting the desired person is often difficult and sometimes requires luck. We all know what's happening in the land of Duce, women are not given the choice to choose to marry the person they love. Men who were attracted to them went to her parents presenting their gifts to make their intentions known. Then, her parents would give their consent and their marriage would proceed without the girl's opinion. I believe in impressions, and the charisma embedded in a lady-which of course I saw in her, I never told her this at the time but I knew someday I was going to.

The next day, standing in my hut, and looking through my window, I saw Rose taking her bath outside just behind her own hut. When she was through, she left and stood closer to the window next to her hut gazing at nature lustfully forgetting that she had nothing covering her body. It was hard to figure out what she was admiring and whirling at, certainly, it was something disturbing from the looks on her face.

Her mind was trapped by the tragedy of her home and had consumed her so badly that the molecules of water on her body had dried without her noticing. She only felt the errant breeze intruding. The breeze wasn't an enemy after all but was merely cruising round to wish the earth well. However, the puzzle of its frustration had caused it to pave its way through to refresh the area in the middle of winter, biting and harsh, this was just one of its bids of nature when it seems so lonely and idle and cares not about the thoughts of human when embarking. Sadly, Rose had wanted not the good of its intentions and hissed at its presence, she lifted her hand and placed on her chest and caressed it gently with her palms and felt a little warmer.

I had been standing at my own hut opposite hers, opening my window and shifting the curtains apart for ventilation. I had forgotten about seeing Rose bathing just when my eyes went over again towards her direction and I spotted her naked. For the first time, I could not let go and I tried not to get caught. My looks rekindled the thoughts and likeness of a woman and I clung forgetfully against my window-admiring and nursing dreams of what I was seeing.

'What a sexy girl,' I commented, bending my head left to right for perfect view. I couldn't resist further seeing her cleavage and her bumpy and puffy breast pointing at me for justice. Our custom had made everything hidden; a man could only see a woman if she was married to him.

'Wow, I wish she rested on my bed, I'll make her breast my pillow,' I spoke to myself aloud; it was not that large but attractive. I had seen it, what lies ahead was how to possibly touch and get hold of it, often, is usually difficult but I was to try. My parents were not that rich to help me get married and until I was able to provide the traditional wine to the family of the lady, I was never to get married to her. I started feeling a sense of wants but the gallon of wine was expensive for me to afford. Our little farm yard planted with vegetable for our daily meal was not enough to exchange for the buying of wine for marriage.

Rose realised she was in the open and saw herself naked, she stretched her hand to grasp her towel; something else caught her eyes; at the entrance into the main gate entering their compound, two cocks were fighting, testing their strength to know who would be able to be the owner of the only hen standing beside. She smiled faintly and wrapped her towel to cover her body. She then raised her head and dismissed herself from the open. It appeared as if our eyes had locked and I thought she had caught me eyeing her nakedness. I was scared and afraid and quickly closed down my window blind so as not to be noticed and was left with a palpitation violent enough to collapse a bridge. Though, she had not noticed anything yet, the guilt on my face was evident as I escaped to my room in shame. That was how I knew her and I began to look for opportunities for our paths to cross for me to air my mind-the little affection I have nursed within, I was not sure if she would accept me but the words of my friends gave me hope.

'You are very handsome,' they would say and each time we went to the village square for dancing in the moon light, girls would always ask me to dance with them. They were big girls and my heart would beat faster for lack of courage. Like every young person, we never stopped experimenting and sexy beautiful big girls would wink at me from time to time, they wanted me to rest on their bed and cover their sheets with them feeling to the very edge of my cuddles but they were wrong because I wanted not their smiles, which seemed so homely to me. Of course I would always look attractive to them but in fact, I was a child with a big size something they would hardly understand because I always used the advantage of my size to dictate my age.

I was only eighteen and have from time to time nursed the thoughts of having an opposite sex with whom I could share intimacy, but not someone older than me, rather someone younger than me or of the same age and my reason was simple, should we get married and grow old, she would still remain appetising. A young boy with an anxiety to taste the realities of life was tied under the slavery of the law. I've never known nor seen the preference of a woman; astonished by what I had seen, my romantic nights began brochures in whirled. The laws of our land were frustrating my dreams and ambitions; I seemed not to care though fear was inside me because I feared our elders and the king.

Rose left and went into her bedroom and it took time for her to dress up; jostled by the problems of her home, when people got closer, more was being discovered and that's how I got to know about it, her elder sister had drank too much wine and went to her room to sleep. The desire to be felt by a man pushed her into masturbation and arousing her own gratification. That same night, Rose's father had had lots of wine too with his friends at the bar. His wife had slept late in cold waiting for her husband to return to no avail. It was customary that, women hardly go to bed without their husband by their side and when they stayed out late, they became concerned, 'what's wrong with my husband, is he alright or in danger,' their thinking would keep them awake, in this case she slept over because she was very tired. When he arrived home, he heard an amusing noise produced by Rose's sister on passing along the corridor to his room, , 'ummmmm, o my god, good, yea' in a seductive tone enough to delectate someone; and, he stopped to check on her, He went into her room and met her naked gratifying herself.

'What are you doing?' he asked above whisper

'Doing ummmm, doing, ummmm, amazing' she replied softly enough to seduce him, caressing gently from her navel down to her clit,

He walked to her to stop her but ended up being the partner for the night and with both of them drunk, they were unable to account for their actions.

The next morning, he left her room to meet his wife in his matrimonial room. She was very angry with him thinking he slept outside without letting her know and they started yelling at each other, the noise woke up Rose's sister and Beatrice stretched lazily and fell off from her bed-making her way to the corridor where her parents stood fraying and told their mother that their father slept in her room.

'In your room?!' she exclaimed,

'You heard me well,' replied Beatrice in a naughty and disrespectful tone, punching her fingers on the thread she held with her and her father stood watching at her in fright, nodding his head sideways in silence and reading through every word she uttered by the shaking of his lips to intercept the hard word. At the time she was confident she wouldn't say it, was just the moment she spoke it out;

'It was not my fault, I was pleasing myself and he walked in, I didn't know what I was doing but I remember that we had sex,' said Beatrice, exposing their little secret.

'You had what?!'Asked her mother in fury- raising her hand and landing her a callous slap on her jaw. Turning behind her, saw an empty bottle of wine and used it to strike the head of her husband, cooup! Squash! Clinkink! The sound of the broken bottle-that could be heard in collision to his head.

She wished she had not ran her mouth seeing her father badly hurt and bleeding and they became so afraid to call their neighbours, scared of the consequences if the truth was discovered. She went to the kitchen, and poured water on to the kettle and placed it on the hearth. When it was hot, she poured it in a bowl and went into the bathroom and quickly picked up a small hand towel hung on top of the toilet door; ran back to the room and dipped it inside the hot water and squeezed it, then used it to clean the wounds of her husband in tears. Rose and her sister stood crying and gazing at their mother in fear.

A neighbour had heard them yelling and called security whom the Duce people called the peacekeeping forces. At once, they came and knocked at their door. Rose went and peeped through the door and saw two of these peacekeeping forces, she ran back quickly and told her mother whom she had seen. She was tensed and shaky and she took a dry cloth, cleaned her hand hastily, and went to the door to see the peacekeeping force, these were the king's police. Looking at her fears, the peace keeping forces requested her husband's presence instead.

'Give me a minute' she said to the peacekeeping forces-rushing to her room to inform her husband, panicking and stumbling as she made her way through.

'The peacekeepers are at the door waiting to see you,' she said to him, trying to adjust his T-shirt, he squeezed the hand towel she was using to clean his wounds and folded it nicely and placed it on his wound and took a cap from his wardrobe and wore on his head

'How do I look?' he asked tapping and adjusting his cap carefully.

'Please hurry, you do not want to waste their time, you do not want to arouse suspicion, do you?' she whispered, pushing him on the back for him to quickly leave the room, exhaling deeply as he left to see them. She wiped her face with her hand and went to the door to meet them there.

'We are sorry,' they said 'we had a call telling us that there was yelling and fighting in this apartment,' said one of the peacekeeper.

'That is ok, we are alright, it's just that my wife was over excited, isn't it? He said turning and looking at his wife for support.

'Yes, of course, family joke,' she groaned, smiling wickedly as she gazed at her husband bitterly.

'We understand, but please try to keep your voice down not to disturb the neighbours, we are sorry again, we misunderstood the information' said the other peace keeping man looking at them intensely.

Blood oozed from the fresh wounds, soaked the towel and started dripping, his wife shifted and stood on the blood and the peacekeeper left without noticing. The peacekeepers were the king's police and by law, they would have faced a community punishment and the husband stripped naked in front of the Duce people and given twenty four lashes and then shot with fruits-humiliating them for the wrong doing with everybody knowing the taboo you've committed, before being reported to the king and your head chopped off. Rose could not be free from walking around the village because anyone who saw her kept their distances, every other person would describe her as the junior sister to Beatrice whom her father slept with. Rose walked down to the park out of frustration to have some time for herself and met this sweet little boy kicking his ball, she joined in and kicked hers and the boy tries to return his own leg of the shorts and fell on the ground.

'Are you ok dear?' she asked.

'Yes!' he echoed and rubbing her hands on his dress to clean the dirty spots, Rose helped him to dust out the particles of dirt on his trouser. It seems as if everything was alright; but the pain had been nursed and the boy did not want to sprout it in the presence of Rose, as soon as she went to pick up the ball for the boy, he burst out in tears and started crying and Rose was concerned.

'I have ruined his pretty smiles and spoilt his day' she thought, and coddled the little boy and took him to his mother who was sitting at the rear of the park, walking to his attention; she then cuddled him and wiped out his tears. She left the park and on her way back home, she heard her name.

Rose! Rose! One of her friends called out to her, she turned and looked at the direction and responded with a smile,

'What are you doing here?' She asked.

'I came to see my uncle' she replied sitting on her horse. 'Come on, let's go' she continued and Rose climbed and sat on the horse and she went with her at the square for them to socialise and make new friends. As they were going, a boy pushed the air giving a particular direction.

'That was my boyfriend, telling me to meet him at a pub up town.'

'Who's that?'

'The guy we just passed' she said pointing behind towards one of the old hut they had passed behind them.

'How did you know he wanted you to meet him there?' asked Rose in desperation.

'One of our secrets, he winked at me and punched at the direction which I understood.' She replied

'Wow, it's nice to understand him that way'. She invited Rose and they both went to the pub. When they arrived, Noella, Rose's friend went and kissed her boyfriend and hugged him and they all greeted themselves and sat down, gave their order for the various drinks they wanted to consume and the waiter brought it to them. I got in to the pub to refresh myself a few minutes later and saw Rose sitting with her friends, I winked at her and she smiled, eyeing at me cunningly, none of her friends knew why she smiled, only both of us were in the game. She stood from her chair in the excitement of my wink and came and met me at the counter-and gave me a glance. I went closer to her.

'My name is Michael, pleased to meet you.' I said.

'I'm Rose Green; I came for some drinks with my friends.' She replied

'I can see that. You look pretty, you know!'

She smiled, and bent her face to the ground swinging her right leg across the other and using her toe to write on the floor. I understood she was interested in what I was saying. My uncle was a womanizer and had told me some of the tactics to know when a woman was giving into your nearness. Some would even harvest grass if the scenario was near a bush and would tear them into pieces repeatedly for the length of the discussion, and for those who were difficult, their smile would mean acceptance. I came very close to her-lifted my left hand up and touched her chin; raising it up a little. She smiled again.

'Are you this shy when talking to someone?' I asked curiously walking closer to her at kissing point.

She did not say a word; she licked her brightly coloured red lips and glanced at me cunningly. I held her right hand and asked, 'Can I take you out somewhere special for us to have some nice time?'

A quizzical expression first fouled her face and she tried to hesitate but I insisted and she accepted with a nod of her head. I smiled and kept drink at once on top of the canter and went to her friends to request for permission. They saw the smiles on her face and granted us the permission and we left from the pub to a restaurant and bought some soup, then, left to a beautiful countryside in west of Duce where we sat and chatted.

I would scoop the soup from the bowl to give Rose and when she opened her mouth to collect it, I would shift it to one side and she would missed the spoon of soup and smile faintly, and I would do it twice or trice for as long as she was able to laugh or smile. I would then use my long fingers to caress her softly. Rose would seize the bowl of soup from me-scoop a certain amount to give me too and when I was about to take it, she would quickly dip it into her mouth and mock me smiling and wagging her tongue to provoke me. The second time she tried to do so; I held her hand and suck out the soup. She jumped on me joyously and kissed me and we both smiled and hugged each other appraising our enjoyable day. After two hours, we parted and left for our homes. We were very happy to have made our friendship and we hoped our relationship would last longer.

'Oh! No! What a ghastly error I've made by not asking this sweet gentle friend where he lives in the village.' Said Rose; flicking her wrist and biting her finger in her hut, we were kind of connected. The pleasure of the moment had consummated our hearts and bridged our smartness, I felt great when with her.

Rose left her hut and rode on her horse to meet her friend Noella in her hut to beg for her assistance on the celebration of-her birthday, for this was very important to her. When she arrived her hut, she knocked the door; her friend recognised her voice and called out

'Rose,'

'Yes,' she answered, 'Come on please get the door open for me,' laughing, and she could hear the crispy voice that echoed excitingly and Noella went and opened it for her; she saw her home messy turned into a play centre by children in the neighbourhood.

'What's going on here?' she asked and the smile she came in with disappeared leaving her with a cold frozen wrinkled face.

'You mean the children?' replied Noella.

'Yes of course! Do you really need to allow them to mess-up your house like this and embarrass you in front of your guest?' she continued,

'You got to be organised, ok,' speaking to the kids and positioning the children to their various seats and cleared their mess. The happiness on the faces of the children evaporated and Noella was not happy. They sat waiting for her to leave for them to continue with their play, grumbling and eyeing at her fearfully. She was that type of girl that would not see things go wrong and pretend as if she was absent, she would obviously do something about it. She was beautiful and a girl of charisma which made up part of her countenances. However, her friend was different, and had her own way of operating, and commented on her behaviour.

'You've just fermented the happiness of these kids my dear. Look how scared they are by your scolding.' said Noella

'what I've done is teach them to live in a clean environ, there is a park outside, they could play there if they want, besides, we need to decide what's wrong or right for them at this stage,' said Rose.

'You've done everything wrong to them just by disturbing their play. Kids are meant to play in whichever environment they find themselves and all we need to do is watch and protect them, guiding them to whatever play they want to engage in because it makes them happy, they grow faster, and while they are doing that, we are supposed to handle them not scold them. I always allow them to play and when they are gone, I then clean their mess. Why do you think they love me so much? My dear, they have few years of this cuddles before being taken by the king to be trained as warriors and you and I know how soon they would-at the age of seven. They are from of warrior descent and the son of a warrior must be a warrior by law. Allow them to enjoy their few years of childhood before being transformed into warriors. Besides this; as a woman, you've got to be careful the way you treat kids, they are believed to be an omen to any woman who hopes to nurse and nurture a child. I'll tell you something that happened to my great grand mum, which qualifies kids to portend good luck to women apart from being a human.

'She was just a woman in her time who could not mother a child and she desperately needed a child of her own. In front of her home was a beautiful garden where children usually gathered to play hopscotch and other games. From time to time, she kept on chasing and chided them from playing in the garden. You know children could be stubborn sometimes and they kept on coming. One Sunday after spending her time and energy to clean and arrange her home, a three year old left the garden and walked into her home with mud prints all over, holding in her arms a doll; she went into her room and placed the dirty doll on her bed. She was in the bathroom bathing, when she came out, she saw the mud prints and traced it to her room and met the child just leaving the room. She stopped her and yelled at her and the child started crying and, she sent her away and flung the doll through the window. Had it been she accepted the child and corrected her in a simple but understanding manner rather than yelling as she did.

'After twelve years, she was still unable to mother a child and had gone to every hospital to get help from the doctors to no avail, she went one day to a traditionalist- a 'native doctor' who specialises in women barrenness and he screed at her predicaments and explained to her,

'Woman' said the 'native doctor'

'You were right you needed a child but your anger swatted the blessing of its coming and the spirits held their peace. She came to you holding in her arms the blessing of your desires and lay on your bed but no, you will not care for her ,instead, you drove her away and flung your fruit over the window but in her were the blessings of your desires and the gods wanted to know if truly you wanted a child. Look woman, it is often said, do not consider the pains of your wounds before taking in medicine less you will take more than required. You acted like that because of the frustration of childlessness and look what it has caused you-all these years of vain hope.' She then understood the action of the kid who brought to her the doll she threw away-and went back in shame and learned from the explanation on how to treat a child as such next time. A few months later as if nothing had happened; the same incidents repeated itself and she handled it carefully and was blessed with the fruit of her womb.'

Rose woke up from her chair and coddled the kids in guilt.

'You just scared the hell out of me by your tale' said Rose and smiling with them.

'I actually wanted you to make me some puff-puff and cakes with some *eru* and bring with you at the party when coming,' said Rose and she left for her home.

Chapter 6

Arriving home, as if I was just waiting, I saw her passing along the street in the quarter I lived and I called her;

'Rose!'

'Hello!' she answered and once again, I could hear the politeness of her tone

'Hello! Forgive me my lady, it's been long since we spoke to each other,' I said to her

'Oh! Mic, how are you? I regretted not telling you where I live in the village last time we met; my world has been cursed with loneliness without you.' said Rose, laughing and I could hear the laughter echoing in the inner part of my ear with lots of excitement and crackled with wit. I booked a date for us to meet and familiarise more for she was in haste and I did not want to take up so much of her time.

For three years, I was able to get to know her well. At times, I would go to the forest and hunt some animals and would pass by her home and give them to her because I was getting interested in her and I saw her as wife material. After some days, I invited her over to my parent's place for dinner and formerly introduced her to my parents. Rose was so happy and loved me the more. On the day she was to meet me at my parent's home, she went and styled her hair and came back home and wore a classy dress to look smart and responsible, of course as you know, it was her first time to come to my home and she needed to create a good impression. I left my house and waited for her at my parent's home in the south with everything set awaiting her. She arrived, and called me, I was standing by, next to where she alighted from her carriage. I walked to her and embraced her and we both rode on my horse towards my parent's home.

'How was your journey my love?' I asked in a lovely tone.

'Very good except for the fact that I'm a bit jittery about meeting your parents, I hope they will like me.' said Rose removing from her bag a tissue which she used to clean her face.

'hahaahahaha! I giggled and gave her a sideways look and said.

'My parents are very jovial and nice, besides, I've told them a lot about you and they desperately want to meet you. You have absolutely nothing to be nervous about. Instead, their patience has been burning since the day I told them about you and they've been longing to meet with you.'

'Thank you my love,' said Rose, rolling her eyes charmingly. The sweet word 'my love' and her charming action triggered pulses of burning affection that shook my heart and glided along my spine which quieted me, I had to remain focused and eyed her from time to time until we arrived.

When we arrived, she removed her jacket and I took it from her and hung it on a pin screwed on the wall on the corridor. I then walked her to the dining table to meet my parents who were there waiting for us.

'Hello my daughter,' my parents greeted simultaneously, standing on their feet and embracing her one after the other, then, they took their seats.

Evelyn, my mum looked at Rose and asked,

'Who are your parents my daughter?' My mum asked smiling in excitement for my choice. She had confirmed in her heart.

'I'm the daughter of Mildred Brook, my mum and Kenneth Brook, my dad and...,' said Rose.

'...Kenneth Brook you said?!' asked Evelyn, the name sounded familiar and her smile escaped quickly to the wilderness.

'Yes of course! Do you know him? Asked Rose

'No! Do you have a picture of him?' my mum asked curiously.

Rose removed from her handbag a photo of her father in black and white and showed my mum. Seeing the photos, she quivered and gasped impulsively. My father Bernard noticed it and muttered; then, gazed at her in discreet silence, I was blind; though I noticed it, I wasn't able to predict the outcome. Only the whining and noise from the food we were chewing could be heard. Rose smiled and appreciated the food.

After we had finished eaten, we went and sat on another chair outside and I told my parents formally that, Rose and I were engaged to be married. They were very happy with my wise decision and my mother, Evelyn, rose, woke Rose up from her seat, kissed her on her cheek and hugged her in excitement. At this time, we were better and our farm produce was encouraging. She stayed for two days in my parent's house-in my former room and later left for her own house confident in the knowledge that my parents had accepted her. She was very happy for the good rapport she had made with my parents.

Two days later, my mother was not herself, at night in bed with her husband; she would persistently nag at her misgivings and was unable to sleep. She wasn't sure but felt something was not right, she went to her secret photos she kept in one of her old bags and removed the photo of Kenneth Brook and gazed at it continuously.

'This shouldn't be happening; it can't be, I love my husband and wouldn't want to nip his world with pain. Why now? I wanted my son to be happy and get for himself the partner of his dreams. However, his choice would bring an era of unforgivable fray,' she thought, pressing her eyes firmly not to water her bed with tears. She was a woman who when things turn against her, you could easily notice by the redness of her eyes and the pool of water down her cheek; this time, she was trying hard to prevent it.

The next morning she rose from her bed, took her bath and went to see her friend Juliana in a town called Murasca in Duce to discuss her problem. When she arrived Juliana's home, she was busy plaiting her hair. My mother knocked at her door and she was ushered in by Juliana. She requested for a glass of water. Juliana gave it to her and she drank it and sat on an armchair.

'What a small world, Juliana, 'she blurted and continued.

'Do you remember the little secret I told you some years back?' she asked.

'Which of these secrets are you talking about? You've shared with me so many of your secrets.' replied Juliana.

'The one concerning my son!' answered Evelyn- shivering down her spine.

'Oh! No! You did not tell me about that one. What's happening?' asked Juliana curiously

'Many years back, I had an affair with Kenneth Brook and he got me pregnant. We knew our lives were at stake so my parents planned for me to have Michael secretly. For over a year, I stayed in our house without seeing the outside. Since the law was tough, we were afraid and did not want anybody to know and report us to the king. No one knew where I was and my family made our neighbours to think I had travelled to the neighbouring kingdom because they kept on asking for me. I did not tell Kenneth that I was pregnant because I never wanted him to get panic and sell himself. Everywhere was dark in the room I was kept in and after some months of extreme darkness, my mum would shift the curtain of my window when she was confident no one would be around to notice me-and the sun would filter through the parted curtain and reflect directly in to my eyes. I would squint to the brightness of the sun and stretch lazily to close the curtain spitting everywhere. This was how we operated until secretly, I was able to give birth to Michael and groomed him until he was two years old. We travelled overnight to the neighbouring kingdom with him and brought him back the next morning. When our neighbours asked us whose child it was, we had to lie to them. We told them that it was a poor orphan I met in the neighbouring kingdom during my visit there. As he was not able to feed himself, I had to adopt him to cater for him. They believed us and we were happy. I left Michael with my parents and travelled again to the neighbouring kingdom to get married since I was no longer a virgin and our tradition forbid people of my kind. The neighbouring kingdom had a different tradition from ours. When I got married, I had to convince my husband to take me back to Duce-my place of origin, he accepted and we rode back to Duce. By this time, Michael was three years old. I wanted to be closer to my son; I had to persuade my husband that I needed someone around to play with since children were not coming sooner. He accepted and asked me if I knew where we could get a child to adopt. I accepted and directed Michael to him. I told him that I adopted Michael in the Brooks Kingdom a year earlier before we got married and he now lives with my parents. He agreed with me and I went and brought Michael as an adopted son. We trained him as our own son-he calls me mother and calls my husband father. When he was eight, my husband and I sat him down and told him that he was adopted. I had to accept it because I never wanted to create a scene though he still took us as his parents.

'You quite remember that, I was one of the unfortunate women who did not get married at an earlier age. I was blessed to be married to him at the age of forty, when menopause was chasing my heels and I had to do something not to render him childless especially seeing how desperate he was to have his own child but he could not because he was sterile. I could feel the pain and did not want to disappoint him. Though like men are; they always point fingers at the women but I knew myself because I was having a child but because I did not want him to feel different. I went back to Kenneth Brook in my fertile period and he penetrated me again I took in his seed and I came back to my home. When I told him that I was pregnant for him, he was very happy and hailed at me with great joy. He was happy with what I said; I gave birth to my second child.' She shook her head left and right and continued.

'I've never told him about the truth concerning Michael and, Michael himself does not know that I'm his biological mother and I don't intend to tell him now. I want to stop this marriage and protect them from committing an innocent abomination. He wants to get married to the daughter of Kenneth Brook. Now tell me, what should I do? I've realised how deep they are in love and I need a perfect plan without them knowing that I am involved in it. Things are gradually falling apart for me and I fear the heart break ahead if he got to know the truth about Michael and his brother.' said Evelyn and sobbing. That was their discussion, when I was still in the dark, how was I supposed to know? I wished I was supernatural to have read her mind and known her thoughts, but no, it was not so, I was in my own little corner stealing her heart and romancing my own sister. It is true what people say, that unknown things refrain us from being hurt, but it wasn't that serious to me until then-when I was surrounded by the 'pennach of known'.

As she was crying, Juliana came closer to her and consoled her; rubbing gently on her shoulder and telling her to stop crying. She then removed from inside her handbag a handkerchief and gave it to her to wipe her tears.

'I think I got an idea, with money everything is possible. I know a girl who will accept to be paid to get pregnant for someone on a contract and when the baby is born, she would agree to go her way leaving the child behind with you without any intention of one day claiming the child depending on the contract you sign with her. She is an expert in dark hours and I know two friends who have had their kids through her, she would not mind locking herself for a year in the dark room just to fill her pockets,' Said Juliana.

'You think so?' asked Evelyn

'I know so,' replied Juliana.

She smiled and embraced the idea and felt better and left to her home. After a day, she embarked on searching for the girl; her name was Luna, to lure her son into sex and getting pregnant for him without loving him. She knew even her son would be scared of raising an alarm because of the law. Moreover, when the baby is born, she would be willing to wave it up and change the town without claims. That was absolutely nonsense and a catch to get hold of me and I must confess my ignorance, I wish I had foreseen what was before me to shy away from its hitch.

Chapter 7

She succeeded to hook up with Luna who took the offer and went into agreement with her. She gave my address to her and told her everything she wanted to know about me. She even advised her of the need for secrecy-and told her to keep the plan earshot from me and I should never know that she was the brain behind the plan. That was my mother rampaging my emotions in secrets to cover her back. Luna accepted the deal and collected the huge amount of money offered to her. She was given two years to complete the deal and leave me alone.

In the cold afternoon of Sunday in winter, places were so chilly and the cold was biting. The rays of the sun were scarce leaving me with frozen frustration that took control of my body making me sneeze and shiver. I was at home sitting and looking up in to the sky via my open widow and admiring creativity. Then I heard a hard knock on the door. I went and peeped via the vent of my door and saw her.

'I don't know this face,' I mumbled twisting my mouth as if seen excrement then readjusted it and opened the door half-way, actually I wasn't expecting anybody.

'Who are you?' I asked rudely but she wouldn't give up at the harsh tone of my voice to refrain from entering my hut.

She smiled and said;

'I'm your neighbour and I'm bored at home alone. I wish to come in and familiarise with you,' she said, which was a good idea, for in that cold day, no one would love to be at home doing nothing if not in the comfort of your bed and the warmness of your wrapper. I was in it and knew exactly how it was like. To me, discussion could breathe out the cold making you excited and feeling warmer.

I gazed at her for a short time and let her into my hut. Since she was a stranger in my home, I had to make her feel comfortable.

'Take,' she gave me a nice packet of pudding wrapped in a clean piece of aluminium foil paper. I took it, opened it in front of her, and started eating it. She would turn and glance at me at every bite her darting down to my manhood -sucking her finger and squeezing her breast gently watching at the whitish water emerging from her erected nipples to attract my attention. At one point, she put her hand in-between her laps, squeezed it, and fingered her clit, removed it, fondling her thigh and caressing her face very softly.

'Ummmmm, this is good' she said softly

I tried resisting the temptation and pretended as if I was not seeing what she had been doing, wishing for her to quickly say good-bye before I opened my mouth to say it lest she says I'm being rude. She persistently seduced me with her actions and it came a point where I could not control myself any longer. There's no doubt about that because I'm human and I have blood flowing in my veins. My manhood stood still fighting its way to the outside hunting her pussy and I went closer to her and held her hand and looked deep into her eyes. She bent her head and kissed me softly, wagging her tongue in my mouth as we continued. The irresistible enticement led us to have sex and I could not belief that I had betrayed Rose, the love of my life and she was the girl I truly love. Luna left after we'd finished and promised to return the next day and I watched her trot out of my house-I was short of words.

Every time Rose planned to visit me, I would make sure I warned Luna not to come around until she had gone. I did not believe myself in a game trying to toy with two women-something I hated but it was real. You should have been there to see how much she loved and cared for me-sacrificing her all to keep us going. She never for once raised her voice at me and we struggled to avoid raised eyebrows. She understood me just the same way I understood her and when she needed attention, she always had a particular charming way of saying it and I would respect the limits.

Whenever Rose was visiting me, she would buy many presents for me and when in my house, she would prepare my favourite food and set it on my dining table for me to eat.

'You are unbelievably romantic, taking time out of your schedule to cook for me, only few unmarried women these days would do that for their men and you make me feel like I am in the ancient days.' I would say to her-smiling and raising my legs and resting them on her laps as we sat on our armchair. She loved it so, and would quickly dip her hands in her bag and remove her blade and used it to trim my toenails, scratching my heels- it tickled me and I would laugh and laugh and she would turn her face and look at me and smile.

'I just love cooking for you Michael, if not all the time but at least creating time like this for it. It makes me feel happy especially seeing you looking at me with those charming eyes' said Rose, and I would shift closer to her and joined my nose to hers showing her too much of my love to keep her confident. She was very happy that she had met her angel and would do anything to make me hers.

After three weeks of my affair with Luna, she got pregnant and told me about it, I was so angry and confused and told her to abort the child. We had a native doctor who gave women concoction to drink if they wanted abortion especially divorced women, she refused and I was very unhappy. She told me to forget about any relationship I was having and concentrate on her and her baby. How she knew I had another relationship remained a puzzle to me because I had never told her anything concerning such. It was difficult for me to comprehend and I drove her away from my hut.

'Get out, you slut,' I rumbled.

I love Rose and would do anything to kill Luna's situation down from been discovered by her. As she walked out, I banged my door in frustration, went, stood closer to my local wardrobe, supporting my forehead with my hand, looking tensed,

'I have taken my own hands and carried fire and it's now burning me,' I said.

Despite so, Luna continued to visit me even though I had declared I would not see her. The little time she had shared with me was making her mad and had made her to develop a strong affection for me. She came to my home one morning when I had dressed-up to go to work and told me to spend some time with her. I was very angry and I ignored her. I sent her out of my house, locked my door and started walking away from the building. She ran quickly ahead of me and stood in front of me;

'Where are you going?' she asked boldly.

'To work of course, where do you think I am going?' I replied angrily while trying to make way for myself.

'I don't think so because if you don't spend time with me today, I will make sure your mother and the entire world hears about this. I'm carrying your child for God's sake and you need to treat me with respect, if not for me, then for the sake of our unborn child,' she roared and turned her back and walked back towards my door and stood there, tapping her foot and vibrating with her hand fixed on her waste. I did not want my mother to know about my affair with Luna neither did I want Rose or the public to know. I never wanted to look irresponsible in front of my parents not to talk of the law. That was before I knew the truth, so I took the day off and went in to the house and spent time with Luna; cuddled her, and enchanted her day with lots of romances.

All these nice qualities in me made her to persistently attach herself to me. She loved me the most. When the day was over, she left to her own house with profound satisfaction. After three months of our discreet relationship, Rose had not discovered anything yet and it gave me the idea that I was getting bigger in the game but like they say-ninety nine days for the thief, one day would always be for the owner. I knew that and was very vigilant.

Rose came to me one evening and told me that, she wanted to move into my house for us to save money towards our wedding. I was confused, she could hardly understand, she turned and looked at me, my face was not bright and Rose responded;

'I was just asking for your opinion but if you are not okay with it, then fine.' She came closer to me and kissed and embraced me with compassion, tears flew down my cheek and fell on Rose's shoulder, she felt it and took her hand and wiped it; then leaned forward and asked;

'Is something bothering you my love? If only I can share the pain of your heart, then let me.'

She said so twisting her face in pity, I coughed and cleared my throat and replied.

'The warmness of your heart keeps me guilty and I wonder if I will cope without you.'

'That's sweet, I'm happy for the love, respect and care you always give to me, the attention; many guys will want to take advantage of me because of my soft heart but you are different and very understanding all the time.' said Rose excitedly; adjusting and unbuttoning her shirt, kissing and holding me closer to her heart and feeling me gently.

'Concerning what you just asked me, I was wondering if you could keep on staying in your home for a while because if you move in with me, I may be bound to open the forbidden door reserved for me after marriage, or what do you think?' I asked while smiling and kissing her gently. She understood, she wanted her virginity to be lost in matrimony and I agreed with her. Could this be the reason for me falling easily for Luna? I was sure because the temptation that day was irresistible to any man in my shoes.

'I agree with you,' she said and continued

'What date do you have in mind for our wedding? I was hoping for it to take place in two years' time, when both of us have saved enough money for the wedding, keeping in mind the other plans to open our own business in three years' time,' said Rose in a gentle tone and smiling curiously to hear from me.

'Great, you spoke as if you were in my mind', I replied.

Rose jumped up from the chair she was sitting excitedly on and fell on me kissing and hugging me in happiness, opening her first two buttons of the shirts she was wearing; exposing her bra and rubbing her breasts on my chest gently. She then passed her hand across my shoulder and around my neck, pulled my head towards her, and kissed me with great excitement. I was very happy seeing her in that great mood and we both romanced each other emotionally. As we continued, the feeling for sex arose and Rose was already giving in but I loved her, I did not want to destroy what she had planned and stopped abruptly and sat back on the chair, Rose was very happy and thanked me; she stood up again and said to me,

'What a marvellous and amazing gentle guy you are, there are many qualities in you yet to be discovered by me, your respect for one's wishes fills me with great passion. I love you Michael.'

'I love you too angel,' I replied feeling honoured, smiling and kissing her. We actually had no respect for tradition and we did things to please us. She was not still comfortable and knew she could trust me and had hope we would be together till death did us part. She straddled and let me in, my tactile and my manly effort splayed her anxiety and she visualised herself at the top of the mountain, honoured by the seven seas, and she felt satisfied. As if that was not enough, I used my hand and snuggled down her body gratifying and causing her to wriggle in excitement; she extended her hands round my loin. Only the endearing murmur and the sound puffing out from the lower angle of her lips could be heard.

'Faster, faster,' she said, felling the sweet slap I smacked on one side of her bottom, remunerating her satisfaction as she entered the hallow heavens. It was easy to notice by the watering of my bed with her squirting. Another line of pleasure extended when my sperms swam down her inside her. A brief silence broke in and a heavy breath blew. A few seconds later, my crispy voice echoed in her ears,

'I hope you enjoyed the match,' I said, wiping her sweat and rubbing through her hair gently. She did not say a word but the gas she passes out signalled me that she was satisfied. It didn't come out intentionally and she feared my reaction. Her mind went cold and snatched the pleasure she was just from having. It was normal for me and she accused me and I accused her and we both used our fluffy pillow to hit each other as we made our way to the bathroom,

'You are a virgin,' I said gently.

It was amazing for me to have slept with a virgin privately, my lover. I said to her the sweetest word of all,

'You don't know how long I've waited to touch your lips, and penetrate your interior.' She smiled and punched me on my chest softly; she has broken the women code for me.

Two days later, Luna was in labour and was laid in the dark room. The dark room was the room kept for females who got pregnant before marriage and their family would try to protect them from the law and would keep them there until they give birth. The child will then be taken overnight to other families in the neighbouring kingdom for adoption. I invited one of my female friends to help me out, when Luna saw me, I don't know what she was thinking but I saw her smile and she turned her back against me as if she was not happy to see me but deep in her heart, she was more than excited and wanted not to be noticed. I walked into the room, kissed her, and gave her the present I'd bought for her. Two hours later, she gave birth; my friend took the neonate, weighed him, and cleaned him up, then brought him to his mother. All this was taking place in my house.

'He looks just like you.' she added and I came closer and carried the neonate; my baby, lifting him up carefully in total joy and looked at Luna with smiles brushing my face.

'I thought you did not want to see me?' said Luna as if she wanted to provoke me. Of course, I did not wish to see her but when it concerned seeing my blood, things had to change and I felt that pulling force attracting me towards my son such that I could not resist it. The fruit of my night labour, he was very sweet and handsome and had hair on his head with a stylish brown colour, I accepted. 'This is my child' I commented. I had forgotten that she asked me a question and I turned to her and said,

'Who said so, not when I'm seeing and carrying my own blood? Thank you Luna for taking this risk despite my rudeness and inappropriate behaviour towards you.'

'That's ok; I knew you would one day recognise me as someone who truly loves you.' She replied opening her mouth in response to what I said. She could not believe I was the one saying it especially with the way I treated her during pregnancy.

I later carried her and her luggage on my camel's back straight to the other kingdom, bought a hut for her and placed her immediately in it. I visited her from time to time to know how they were faring, cooking and caring for her though keeping my footsteps secret from Rose, her parents or people who knew me. I had a very good rapport with Rose's parent and occasionally they invited me for dinner at their house and took me out for fishing, sometimes I even slept over at their house and her father respected me and entrusted his daughter to me with confidence. It wouldn't be fair if they saw me with another woman and at the same time I couldn't change the fact that I've used my bare hands to pick up fire.

After a week, Evelyn went to see Luna; she knew everything going on and quieted herself praying for her plan to work. She bought things and took along with her to visit Luna. When she arrived, she congratulated her for the good job she was doing and Luna pledged to be loyal and stick to her plan. As they were still discussing, I rode in with my horse and my mother saw my horse through the window, alerted Luna and she showed her the way out through the back door and she used it and went out just before I could walk in to the building. She rode away with her horse to her home smiling confidently about how progressive her plan had gone. You could say I was naive not to have noticed what was going on but I could never have imagined that my mum could plot such evil against me knowing the truth and decide to hold it back from me. That was then, I was with a sack of food items and went and kept it in the kitchen and was expecting appraisal as she usually did when I bought her something but received none. I went closer to her and realised that her face was not bright and she was very sad and perturbed,

'What's bothering you my dear?' I asked coldly.

'You of course, what do you take me for? I've been carrying your child for the past two weeks and none of your family have bothered visiting me, you yourself have not introduced me to any of them, you are making me think that I'm not been recognized by you or your family and...'

'You are getting this wrong, I have plans in place but you just need to be patient and let things work out perfectly for our own good!' I said to her in a loud and convincing tone, walking towards her and rubbing her jaws with my hands with passion and claws of hanky-panky emotions to make her comfortable and free, knowing that I love her. Really, I detested her attitude. She was pushy, bossy and authoritative and felt less about my opinion and feelings, and cared only about her wants and needs. I never told her any of this and hoped not to but pretended to exhibit true emotions towards her; however, my son was key to my nearness to her. Luna had fallen in love with me, I noticed and she intended not to lose me to anybody and would do anything to prevent it from happening.

Six months to our wedding, I had begun buying some essential wedding items bit-by- bit and my mother noticed it in a visit to my home. She went straight to Luna and pressurised her to add more efforts in stopping me from marrying Rose. She told her about my seriousness and mentioned the items I'd bought for her, she shook her head and said;

'Your son is stubborn but I think I've got another idea to ruin his marriage plans with Rose.'

'Whatever thing you are planning must be quick and hasty because time is running out,' said my old woman.

She left Luna's home to go to her home feeling a little relief by words from Luna. A week later, Luna went to Evelyn's house uninvited, she was at home with her husband when she got a knock on her door. She went to open it and saw that it was Luna; her husband was closer and she asked,

'Who are you my daughter? Shivering and panicking in frustration. Luna noticed it and replied,

'I'm Michael's friend'

'Oh! Come in, Michael has many friends and they usually visit us.' She smiled and Evelyn walked closer to her and whispered in her ear,

'What are you doing here?' in cold anger

'Part of my plan' she whispered confidently and Evelyn whispered to her again,

'I hope you know what you are doing,' in doubt and fear, trembling as she walked her to her husband for introduction. He was happy to see her, it appeared as if it was not the type of Michael's friend that have been visiting them when Luna told them about her relationship with me and about the son we had,

'A son!' they exclaimed

'You mean my son has a son and didn't bother to let us his parents know about it? What have we done to him, how can we protect him from the king's wrath if he denied to confide in us?' said Evelyn in surprise.

My father was very angry and disappointed with me and sent for me immediately. I've hardly had such an emergency call from my father, and knew within myself that something was wrong with my father. I got in to my horse and rode to my parent's home. When I arrived there, my eyes first went on Luna; my spirit was broken and I trembled in guilt, I knew how flippant she was and I was scared for my life. My father lifted up his head and spoke to me, reminding me of the law,

'Michael! I feel so disappointed in you. You know how much we your parents love you and you decided to treat us with disrespect. How shameful it is to have a son and hide him from your parents, we are supposed to be the one to protect you. How could you trust others than us your parents? Are you insane? What if they had betrayed you? I guess you know the consequences,' he said pulling himself from the tight chair he sat on and walked to his backyard. I sat down in shame sobbing. Luna could not resist the scene; she stood up, promised to take the child along with her when next she was to visit them, and left. My mum felt my pain, came closer to me, and comforted me.

'Mum, will you ever forgive me for my stupidity? I was very naive to have taken such a decision, please help me beg father to understand my fears- the good son I have always been which led me to hiding my child from you people. Please mum; whatever the case, don't tell Rose, make father to understand!' At that time, I was not even thinking about the consequences, all I thought of was Rose and the love I had for her.

I went behind the yard, apologised to my father and left. to my home. Luna came to me a few minutes later after I had left my parent's place and I did not bother to attend to her, she sent me a written message saying,

"I'm sorry Michael, you did not give me the attention I needed, I followed you secretly to know where your parents lived. I'm very sorry, I just want to be part of you-a woman to be loved and cherished. I want to have you with me forever-wake up every morning and see your smile, cooking for you and making you my toy. Please don't be mad at me"

I did not even reply to the message and tore it immediately, hissing and twisting my face during tearing. Back in my parent's home, my mother's heart was bubbled with anger and frustration and she was unable to comprehend the type of love I had for Rose that I was not willing to let go despite her efforts. She later was sober and wondered if the plan would work at the end, she was not willing to give up; she knew it was hurting me but she had no choice and had to prevent siblings from getting married at all cost.

'Should I just tell them the truth and stop being a sadist to my children? No, if my husband got to know about Michael, it would hurt him to death to think he trusted a devil. Not now, I want a stable home and must break up my children in secret no matter what it takes, period!' she thought.

Two months came and passed, Rose came to me to find out from me what items I had purchased for our wedding. I was in my bedroom resting and Rose woke me from my bed and we walked to the sitting room together; winking and glancing at each other with affection-holding hands tightly. She had a beautifully coloured lipstick on her lips with nicely styled hair and was looking beautiful and glamorous. I threw myself at her to ease the pain and stress I was into. Allured by my smiles, Rose pulled me to herself, kissed and caressed me gently in happiness and we had another round of sex.

She stood up and adjusted her skirt, went to the kitchen and made some food and we sat and ate it with smiles, kissing and cracking jokes with each other. When we had finished eating our food; Rose told me to take her out for a walk, I accepted and we went to the bath and bath then dressed up and went out together walking majestically on the pedestrian lane with each other's hand around the loin of each other, bouncing and adjusting our footsteps as we paraded.

Across the lane was a market, she urged me to accompany her to the market and I accepted and we went inside.

'Wow!' I exclaimed looking at a nice pair of shoes

'Do you like it?' asked Rose holding and gazing at the shoe properly.

'Yes baby' I replied softly.

Rose picked the shoe, put it in her shopping bag, added some few items in her bag, and paid for it. I also bought a pair of sandals and knew Rose would like of it, hid it behind me without her knowing. I helped her to carry the items placing the sandals inside quickly for her not to notice as we walked back home.

I removed the sandals when we arrived home and presented it to her and she was surprised and jumped in excitement, thanking me for buying her beautiful and expensive sandals. It was normal for me because I always get the word each time I get something for her.

After two months, I visited Rose, carrying with me a bag of fruits. I met her in grief weeping and wearing in thoughts. I rushed to her and asked after her problem.

'What's the problem Rose?' I asked curiously.

'I have been sacked from work,' said Rose in tears and her eyes were red and dim and her runny nose exaggerated the pain she was into.

'But... why?' I asked while trying to console her.

'The manager said, he wanted to reduce staff due to the financial difficulties of the bakery. I was amongst those sacked. Said Rose turning and hugging me and sobbing. There was something more to it and I could see it in her eyes though she was not prepared to discuss it and I did not want to bother her especially seeing her in that painful state.

I slept over at her place because I did not want to leave her alone in her pain. Four days later, she wrote to me telling me that she now had another job working as a nanny. She never told me whom she was working for and I did not bother to ask.

Luna's mother was involved in an accident and was badly injured. She was rushed to the hospital. She was shocked by the news and - her mother being the only parent she had- was unable to withstand the feelings she got for her and stayed back without visiting her. She employed the services of Rose to rush and see her mother in the hospital. Her mother was not aware of her son and the job she engaged in and she did not want to embarrass her mother by taking her son along with her.

When she arrived, she gave her instructions on how to run her home in her absence.

'In the morning when the baby is asleep, make sure you clean the house and wash his used dresses and dry them on the line, his food is in the upper cupboard in the kitchen make sure you feed him. He eats five times a day and make sure you give him food within a two-hour interval. These are the things you will use to bathe him with and his oils are in the cupboard beside my bed and there is food in the kitchen in case you need some.' Bla- bla- bla, and she took the instructions and Luna left to see her mother at the hospital.

I closed from my work and took a drive to Luna's place to check on them buying some food items, when I knocked the door, Rose came and opened it and we were both surprised to see each other there

'Michael! She called

'Rose! What are you doing here?' I asked curiously walking in to the house in derange. It escaped my mind that she was now a nanny.

'I'm working; I was about to ask you the same question.' said Rose; trying to figure out my mission in Luna's house.

'I am on an errant for my boss, where is Luna, his wife?' I asked frowning faintly.

'She went to see her mother and...' said Rose

'...Without telling her husband?' I asked in a perturbed tone

Rose turned and gazed at me,

'Why do you sound like you care?

'No! Do I? Because, he should have told me, he actually said I would meet his wife at home. All the same; nice to see you at your work place, I said; kissing her softly and dropping the items in the kitchen and left immediately for Rose not to suspect anything. I wrote to Luna to inquire why she had to leave without informing me, I never made her to discover Rose had something to do with me. I drove home exhaling deeply. She apologised to me in a message.

Luna spent three days with her mother at the hospital and when she was discharged, she returned to her home, placing her under care. Rose's duty in her home ended. She stopped by my place and prepared me some food. She went to her hut in Calinia north of Duce kingdom. She had left a note to inform me that she called around the house. When I came home, I saw the place cleaner and tidier than I had left it before I went for work. I surveyed my house, went to the kitchen and saw a delicious meal had been prepared for me. Who could have done this, I wondered. I became confused and knew within me that, Rose was the only person who had the key to my house but was scared because Luna would do anything to surprise me; after all, she went to my parents' house without me leading her there;

'Maybe it is her own little way of bribing me so that, I do not become angry because she left to see my parent without my knowledge,' I thought.

I went into the kitchen, dished myself a portion of food and sat on my dining table to eat. My eyes went towards the direction of my wardrobe and I saw a piece of paper; I went closer, picked it up, read it and smiled knowing the real cook. A day later, Rose sent me a letter to verify if I was home and had noticed what she had done. I laughed as I read the letter and appreciated her effort and thoughtfulness for passing by my home in my absence.

The next day, Luna sent a message through her friend and told me that she was home and wanted me to buy some items for her at the market and bring them to her house. I agreed and left for the market and bought the items she requested and took them to her house. When I arrived, I dropped the items in the kitchen, went to the sitting room, and saw Luna bathing our son, laughing and cuddling him, kissing and touching his cheek. It was charming the way she did it, the baby would smile and laugh loudly wriggling and writhing in excitement. I stood at one corner looking at him and smiled too.

Luna raised her head up and looked at me and said,

'If only you could look right deep into your son's eyes and see his innocence- a child who needs a father besides him always, to hold and care for him with passion, watch him play and grow; carry him in warm arms feeling his cuddles and protection. He came a long way from wonderland to belong and be loved by us and I think we should respect his wishes for choosing to be born by us and live together as a family, as one forever –nursing and caring for him.'

I was short of words and looked at her in bewilderment. Her words went deep into my heart. I went closer to her, kissed, and hugged her with a little pity and affection, nobody needed to advice on how to take care of my son. I realised I was lacking something and her words made sense to me. I joined my head with hers understanding her desires and wishes to be married to me. I kept it to myself, stayed with them for a while, and left to my home.

A few days later, I went to see my parents hoping their anger towards me would have subsided and I would be able to proclaim my new development. I met them the way I had hoped. They were sitting in the front yard on the corridor. My father was sitting on his traditional armchair and my mother sat on a bench opposite his. I greeted them, went in, and kept my cargo removing a gold chain I had bought for my mother and a gold bracelet I bought for my father and presented it to them smiling. They were so happy and thanked me for my generosity, I was very happy. Evelyn took the chain to her husband to wear it on his neck and he did and she saw that it was good; she kissed her husband and hugged me joyously. I looked for my own chair and came outside, sat down and said to them,

'Mum, dad, I have reconsidered my plans and I want to get married to my son's mother.' I said expecting their objections, they knew Rose too well to just let her go like that and there were some things my father did not like about Luna but the fact that she was mothering my son warmed his heart towards her.

'Why Michael?!' asked father and Evelyn coincidentally focussing on me. My father continued:

'Do you love her? He asked looking directly into my eyes.

'Father, I don't know if it is love or wanting to take responsibility for my son....'

'What about Rose, do you still love her?' asked Father, gazing at his wife for support. She nodded her head in support of the questions but right deep in her heart was a bubbling anger to prevent her husband from causing me to change my mind.

'I'm in love with two ladies but there is a side of Rose that I can't resist, the affection keeps on pulling me towards her and I don't want to destroy her future. The deed has been done and I want to take responsibility for my actions,' I said sounding so disturbed, my mother probed further

'My son, follow your heart and rest in the comfort of your responsibilities and dignity. If you are sure of what you've just said, then, I can help you talk to Rose. She will be heartbroken but she will definitely get over it and understand. I am proud of her for a firm and compact decision to preserve her womanhood until this time of her life. It's a challenge most women of this age wouldn't venture in.' When she mentioned her womanhood, I bent my face to the ground, they could not understand but I guess you do and I was glad that my father had wrestled the grudges he had against Luna.

Father kept quiet and said nothing more; they continued drinking their wine and enjoyed the errant breeze that blew past their yard.

Evelyn invited Rose out for a dinner two weeks later; telling her my heart and, secrets I had kept from her; she was so angry she left her at the table and went to her home without uttering a word. She respected my mother and did not want to do anything stupid. She was unable to concentrate and words of my mother kept repeating themselves in her mind; she went into her carriage and drove to my place to find out for herself.

That day, I was sitting on my chair when she barged in to my house, I woke up to know what the problem was,

'Is it true what your mother told me?' asked Rose tapping her leg on the ground repeatedly.

'What did she tell you?' I asked, I never knew that my mum had told her as we agreed at my parent's home. I walking closer to her to sedate her animosity. She slapped the hand that I placed on her shoulder and shifted to another position.

'About your child and marriage to another woman,' Rose continued.

'I wanted to tell you this a long time ago but it was difficult for me. Everything my mum told you was the truth but she was the one who lured me into copulating with her- I was sitting in my house before she came...' I said, thinking it was enough to get her attention. I knew it was nothing to make her forgive me; if I were in her shoes, I wouldn't even stand to listen to the trash I was saying to her. I would have given her a slap before turning my back and walking off. No, it wasn't like that with her; she had the patience to listen to me and I had the guts to think I could explain to her. Well with love, everything is possible.

'Who is she?' asked Rose

'Luna...'

'Luna! So that day you came to her house was not a coincidence, you lied to cover your back right?' she asked with tears running down her cheeks. I couldn't say a word and felt the pain she was going through but I had made my decision and wanted my son to grow up with his parents.

'I've been a fool to have trusted you. You don't know how long I've wished and hoped to sleep by you, waking up every morning and see your smiles, kissing you and telling you good morning. Why Michael? Have you forgotten so soon, the love you promised me? You always sang love songs to me, cuddling me like a baby, holding me in your warm arms and watching over me as I slept and told me a million times the amount of love you had for me. Your affection drowns my thoughts and everywhere I went, in the crudeness of the sun; I want to sleep in your arms but right now, the anger of your betrayal has left me in this state of patency. Why my love? Did you do that because of my softness and respect for you? said Rose in agony, crying and leaning against the wall. She appeared enervated by me and exhausted by her woes. I drew closer to her again and hugged her trying to calm her down but she wouldn't stop. She slapped my hand, pushed me to the floor, scattered everything in my hut then left my house, went into her carriage and drove off. When she arrived home, she got in to the house, kicking places in frustration and annoyance. Then, she picked up a card I gave to her and tore it into pieces, blubbering and rolling on her floor in agony. She could not believe she had been dumped by the person she had trusted and sacrificed so much for. At once, the thought of failing to disobey tradition sprang right deep in her mind and she felt the gods were punishing her. She wrote to her friend Noella and informed her about her break-up with me. She was surprised and drove to Rose's house to find out more about the cause of our break-up. She told her and was unable to control tears from running down her cheek; grasping Noella's hand tightly and trying to stop herself from crying.

Noella drew closer to her and patted her shoulder begging her to be calm,

'You see Rose; love is a tray of water that can evaporate with time. The love Michael nestled you with had blunted and to see you wallow in this pain makes me weak. You just have to give up and hope to find a soul mate one day who will truly love you for who you are,' said Noella with a convincing tone to comfort and make her feel relieved.

'You think so?' asked Rose, biting her fingers softly to absorb the shock of rejection. Noella went in and prepared something for her to eat, she ate a little, and she encouraged her to forget the incident and move on. She then got in to her carriage and drove to her home.

Four months later, Luna moved into my house and started living with me. Evelyn had not been informed. She went to the market and bought her son a nice dress and came to my home to surprise me with it, and met Luna. She went in to the kitchen and brought to her a bottle of fresh water; poured it in to a cup and gave it to her- smiling and winking at her, she reciprocated in different notion, blinded from what she was yet to discover. After thirty minutes of resting, she was served food and as she was dining, Luna went to the table and said,

'Michael and I have agreed to get married'

She spat the food in her mouth on to the floor.

'Repeat what you've just said' said Evelyn furiously, frowning and shifting her plate of food away from her. She gripped the cup of water kept in front of her and sipped it; using it to rinse her mouth then asked,

'I hope you realise the implication of what you have just said. He mentioned this to me last time but I did not take it seriously because I have confidence in your actions and to hear you say that, pisses me off,' said Evelyn.

'I do understand and know the agreement I signed, but it would be unfair to deny what my heart truly wants. Mum, I'm willing to give you all the money you paid to have me know your son. He is a wonderful person, someone whom I have gotten to know and grow to love. You and I know how much we've hurt him and made him denounce his true love, let's not deny him his responsibilities again especially when he has fully made up his mind to do so.' said Luna

'Enough! I do not need the money and your sermons, what I need is for you to free my son from blackmail and stop luring him in to infatuations;' said Evelyn, raising her eyebrows.

'Then you leave me with no choice than to tell your son about the role you've played in his separation. I guess you wouldn't want to contain his fury and the exasperation of your husband,' said Luna, walking gently to her room. Evelyn shook her head in disappointment, looking intently at her until she disappeared. She had no option left, hearing her annoying words, stood up and seized her handbag to her chest adjusting her bead and opened the door and was about to leave. I met her at the door; she smiled and went back with me inside, and presented her gift to me though not sounding as happy as she did when she came in to the house in the beginning. The sight of Luna disgusted her. Without wasting time, she saluted me and went away to her own home.

Ten days after their fray, I called my parents informing them about the date I had set for our marriage. The news about our wedding flew to Rose's ear, she tried to control her emotions accepting the fact that I was getting on with my own life, and she needed to do the same and stop wallowing in her frustration.

'I'm pregnant for Michael and he is with another woman, with a son. No, this can't be happening to me. I hate you Michael and I won't show you your child for as long as I live. You disgust me.' Rose sat thinking and whispering aloud.

I did not tell Rose about our wedding nor did I invite her to it. We never wanted to raise an alarm and for her to come and cause a scene would cause the law to hunt us. We travelled overnight to the Brook kingdom, which had a different tradition from ours and made it easier for people of my calibre to get married. This was the only way we used to trick the law not to grip our heels.

In the Brook kingdom, during marriage, their elders would gather in a large hall. The couples would move forward covered with a large cloth so that no one would see them while in the hall. Then, the elders would walk up to them and they would stretch their palms forward and open them wide and one by one, their elders would spit on their palms and throw little earth on them. This was their own way of blessing them. When the elders had finished, the parents of the couples would move forward and unveil the couples and the rest of the people would clap. The couples would rub their hands and feet with the spittle, then they would eat and drink until the day was over.

On the day of our wedding, she came and sat at the back. The elders performed the marriage rites and at one point, he stopped and asked if anyone has anything against the couple that they felt they should not get married? The elders paused and looked up to the congregation for their opinions. I was examining and flicking my eyes at the population, smiling, then our eyes met and light reflected from Rose's necklace; I squinted my eyes a little to verify if she was the one. I had not invited her. Where and how did she get to know about this day in my life? I hoped she had no intention of ruining it. I cleared my throat with the fright of what she might say-keeping me panicky and sweaty. Luna could not understand and removed the handkerchief from my inner pocket and then wiped my sweat gently and, turned my face towards her. It did not matter to Rose at all and she said nothing. When the five minutes given for opinions were over, I took a deep breath and, the priest completed the rites. We kissed each other and the merriment went on from the church premises to our home until we were all drunk.

After our wedding, we sat opening the various gifts given to us. Luna came across a beautiful parcel attractively designed and decorated. She showed me and when we opened it, we saw a golden chain addressed to Michael in an envelope with a short note in side. I quickly squeezed the note into my palms so that Luna will not look at it because I was not sure of the content. I knew the writing. When she tried to ask, I told her that it was just a label and she didn't bother to ask further because she believed me. On the note, Rose had written telling me she was the one who gave the gift waving her passion and reminding me of the love we once shared. I left Luna in the parlour and went to my room to read the note, which read,

'It was hard to see you in the arms of another woman, but my love for you has never faded and my heart kept on beating faster each time we looked at each other and I know you cannot pretend not seeing the blood oozing out of my eyes with passion hoping to have you by my side. It is true that you have made your choice which is why I would like to wish you well in your marriage and congratulate you for ruining the trust we bore for each other, the bond we shared and the promises you failed to realised,' she wrote and signed with her tears. When I read it, I tore it into pieces hiding the content from Luna but felt the words and absorbed my emotions to stop them from sprouting outward and creating suspicion. After we had finished opening our wedding gifts, I wrote to her but she never replied.

I actually was asking her something, there was a part of her note that said,

'There is something I would like to embarrass you with, maybe in a year's time, may be in twenty years or never but I hate the sight of you,' she would not give me the chance to after all I am a married man and she was keeping her distance.

Chapter 8

Sixty months later, I went to see the doctor. I was feeling constantly drowsy and could not quite understand how all of a sudden I'd become so sleepy. Was I suffering from sleeping sickness? Of course, I was not in a position to answer that question. I went to the doctor, he suspected it from what I told him but was not sure and passed me through a scan and discovered the undiscovered. I was diagnosed with a very serious, double form of cancer - leukaemia and brain tumour,

'Cancer?! I cried aloud hopelessly, tapping my laps and looking into nothingness. I felt the pain eating through my marrows and myself so empty and weak to support myself. I knew the end has come. I had only just heard the word- cancer, and started thinking of the worst. Thinking straight for me at that time was a nightmare and living became a fantasy I was pursuing. I wished I had not gone there but it was a step towards betterment; to know the unknown was hard. I know people who had the illness and how they suffered with it. Then like the bird, I could hear the soft and gentle words of the doctor echoing and filtering through my ear and ringing in motion, telling me,

'It's hard we know, knowing the truth about you helps us help you and gives you a better chance, I'll do everything in my power to see that the symptoms are better managed.' The doctor was very friendly though, I could not help myself and moment after moment, my face was wet with tears. That is true, I had to accept it, I have cancer. Further appointments with him saw that it had corrupted my system beyond repair and the doctor had told me that I had barely three years to live and decided to place me on strict medication. What I needed was able to care for me. The attitude of my wife after knowing my predicament consequently adhered mockery and I become lonely, but why did I have to, why did I chose home care, was I wrong to rest in the comfort of my family? She began dating another man in secret. I had chosen home care knowing I would be catered for and loved by my family. I had no idea until I discovered it.

Christopher as they called him was a renowned drug addict feared by the community; it was funny that the law saw it right and gave him constant privileges. Christopher had a written part of him far from printing - when he was a child, in a struggle for a plate of corn with his sister; he got his sister knifed to death. The love his parents had for him was so strong that in spite of the pain he had caused them, they were willing to saving him. They gave him a new identity and sent him to a different town. He lived right beside me and preyed on forbidden goods that our law ignores. She wanted his money, to be able to live the luxurious life she had always hoped for; splashing and lavishing money the way it would please her. For me, I value my hard-earned money so much and would only use it when necessary, which was contrary to Luna's thinking - a girl who has just emerged from the terrors of poverty and has missed so much in life wouldn't want opportunities to pass by. On several instances, she had tried to spend my money carelessly and I cautioned and calmed her down reminding her of the need for modesty but the event of my illness exploded her nonchalant attitude that infuriated me. I saw her as being archaic to societal realities knowing her background, and knowing my condition, where she came from; a beautiful girl from an impecunious home who engaged in prostitution just to make sure she fed her family. Things changed drastically for her, she lacked the patience to build her life before starting to live the extravagant life she had always wanted. To her,

'Life is short, if I don't live today what would I do tomorrow when the its unpredictable bells ring.

On a night out to a party nearby, she met with him and Christopher saw her as a perfect romantic angel. He approached her and made his intentions known to her. From thence, every night became busy for her and she always had reasons for sneaking out to meet Christopher at his home. Before she went, she'd remove her ring and keep in her cupboard beside our bed. I was not happy, she changed and started visiting him very early in the morning.

'Where have you been?' I asked looking directly into her eyes.

'What sort of question is that? Didn't I tell you that I was going out for sport,' she answered, dodging my gaze so that I would not to be able to see her guilt.

'Sport you said? Leaving the house at 6:00am in the morning for sport and only returning at 1:00pm in the afternoon; what sort of woman are you that you don't even have an iota of respect and care for our son or me your husband? I had to call off my therapy to look after the baby. What is the essence of having you as a housewife? We were supposed to support each other but you are failing to fulfil your responsibilities. You are not the Luna I got married to; a lot has changed since we started living together. You were very caring and lovely and the only thing that I saw wrong with you at that time was your arrogance and authoritarian way of life; subjecting everyone to your bidding which I thought I could manage but today, you are getting worse and unreasonable. I do not want much from you; all I ask is for you to be the mother and woman everyone will appreciate and respect. Be the woman that when I'm gone even to the land of the dead, I will be proud of - knowing that I entrust my son in the arms of someone who can care and protect him. You once told me about the love of a father for his son; now, I urge you to do the same and be the mother of your son. My days are numbered and I don't want to take a decision that I will regret when I'm gone in the land of the dead.' I said to her and allowed her to reflect on what I had said. Luna stood with her hand on her waist, then, she left to the bathroom and had her bath then returned into the hut and carried our son, cuddling and singing affectionate songs to him. I stood watching them and I thought right deep within me that, my words could have changed her and possibly mean something to her.

Bullshit, damn it, she practically continued with her sport despite what I had said to her and the rate at which she went out this time around got me concerned. She always left the house early in the morning only to return in the afternoon. I took a step to track her and to know the type of sport she always went for that occupied her that long and saw her entering the radical- Christopher's house. I returned to my house with my suspicions confirmed. When she came back home, I did not ask her anything like I used to before and only swallowed the anger and pain of betrayal to be digested by the enzymes of courage and comfort to keep my mind thoughts free. Her connection with Christopher got her into drugs and alcohol and she became addicted .

Every blessed day, I kept on weeping and saying to myself aloud, pounding my hands through the air,

'I must survive, I must survive,' leaning on an oak tree in my garden, why me? I questioned myself several times and felt a sharp pain hooking my ribs to a standstill, I stopped my breath for some few seconds for the pain to run through and relieve me. I couldn't understand what was going on and on

102

the other hand I thought my internal organs were reacting to my predicament. It was hard for me, not only with the illness I have been diagnosed with, but the fact that I was uncomfortable in the arms of my family and guilty in the terrain where I was supposed to be comfortable. I needed someone to talk to me, someone to encourage me and make me feel there was hope. A few minutes later, I felt my heart beat faster; I became afraid and feared to encounter the worst high blood pressure, it was not something I could be proud of with my illness in me. I left the oak tree and ran round my garden three times to distract and free myself from thinking and it appeared to be working. I found myself going back to the memory of when I was five, the things I use to do and the love my parents showed me, everything I asked was given to me. It was funny because they would always satisfy me before themselves and I always wanted it so- a transition between my id and ego. I felt this sweet loving and beautiful smile coming from the depths of my heart; you could see my mouth expanding wide as I smiled. It was rare for me and I was almost forgetting what I had in me. I turned around and saw a sweet lady sitting in the garden next to mine smiling and waving her hands in my direction, my smile escaped quickly from me, I couldn't explain what was going on with me, but I could understand I was filled with obsession,

'Oh my God, I had started hating people without them doing anything to me.' It was as if anything anyone did was mocking me; it was not true because she was trying to be friendly. I cried and begged my heart, 'don't do this to me,' I cried. A fresh wind blew and whipped my hair across from left to right and I summoned happiness from within me to smile back at her and before I could make that decision, she had gone closer to another guy and was chatting with him. I hoped she had understood me, understood the pain I was going through. I got angry and left the garden to my home.

I went and complained to my mum about Luna's behaviour and she was so unhappy but reserved her comments. Luna's mother did not know about her baby until the day of her wedding when she left from the hospital in the injury she sustained in an accident. When I told her about her daughter's recent attitude, she called her and cautioned her but she would not listen and continued to mess up her life though I did not tell them about her affair with Christopher but highlighted the rate at which she went for sport and the time she returns which to me was wrong. Every family needed to have their own secrets.

My mum came to our home when I was not, and, attacked Luna for maltreating both her son and grandson, urging her to be of good behaviour towards them. However, she got blackmailed by her and fearing exposure, she had no choice but to leave. With she realised the mistake she made by bringing Luna into her family. It seems she had made a ghastly mistake based on deceit and blackmail, what was she to do? She herself was not sure and swirled in confusion as she stumbled into her sitting room. Her husband rose quickly to catch her from falling; bumping into the side stool next to the table as he made his way through, and both of them fell on the ground. He smiled and kissed her and seeing her husband smile, she switched her mood and pretended to be happy. But, the thought kept on coming,

'Kenneth had no history of cancer as the doctor told me but I do not understand why Michael was so unfortunate because even I was free from such. Could it be the gods are punishing me?' Evelyn sat at home wondering; the thought of losing her son was a major problem to her.

Rose went to a party her friends had organised; she sat at the rear and saw a guy at the corner staring at her. She pretended not to see him and continued to whoop in excitement as the party cake was being cut. She turned again and glanced at him, and saw his eyes resting fixedly on her face assessing and winking at her. She rose and walked outside to test his seriousness-he followed her too and went outside, and had a chat with her. Rose knew his sister and brought her name into their conversation to prolong their discussion. When she noticed he was not coming out clear with his intentions, she tapped his jaw softly and went inside after prompting him to say his mind to no avail. Wilson was not clear, he had come out to say something to Rose about what he felt seeing her but the words escaped from his heart and mouth and he found himself blushing and chatting deviations to his interest. 'What exactly was I to say?' he thought, tapping his leg on the floor and looking at the stars, flipping his finger as he walked back into the party hall. At least he had hope knowing her name and knowing that she knows his sister and they were friends even though that was not a guarantee.

Two days later at 3:00pm, he went to Rose's house, she was surprised to see him and asked who told him where she was lived,

'I got your address from my sister though she was not willing to give me; I had to trick her before collecting the information from her' he said

'It's rude of you to come to my home uninvited,' she replied tensely feeling the prickle of her hair as it rested on her neck, she shook her head and adjusted it then reconsidered and ushered him into her house and they engaged in a conversation;

'I knew this was what you were driving to when we met at the party but I really wanted you to come out plain and now you have,

'What do you see in me that attracts you if I may ask?' she asked while pouring wine into his cup gently giving him an ample view of her cleavage causing him to look forgetfully at her breasts; she noticed it and stopped pouring the wine and sat beside him asking about his prospects.

'Everything,' he said grinning

'Everything you said! Why did you say, everything? As far as I know, guys go for a lady because something in her hits his heart and not everything. From what you have said, you are trying to tell me that I am perfect, and I don't believe you. I, as a human must have my own limitations and weaknesses, now tell me again dear, what in me attracts you?' she asked while laughing and scratching her head and pulling strands of her hair towards her chest and twining them to form a rope.

'Everything' he replied again, sipping his wine gently and continued.

'When I said so I mean it, love hunters would tell their partners how much they love them for their beauty, intelligence, attitude and more but what happens when these qualities are no longer there? Let me be straight, I am not here to deceive you neither am I here to gamble. I have been a victim of heartbreak and I have realised that when you find a reason for loving someone, you'll thus have a reason for hating that someone and the circle continues with impairment, which has rendered so many people like myself separated. That's why I said everything; everything in the sense that, if I have no reason for loving you then I will also have no reason for hating you. I love you Rose and I want everything possessed by you to make me whole and complete. I want to think of your smiles on a beach on a sunny day with the rays reflecting and spying on our romance and both of us burying ourselves right deep into the sand like crickets- diving in to the sea and sipping its saltiness, spitting it out and kissing each other. Or, a fray that leads to cuddles and pampering that would make us forget our lonely past and command us into a love not felt before.'

'Stop, she interrupted

'Why are you making me feeling guilty by implying that not loving you would be a mistake?' said Rose holding her hands close to her chest and twisting her face in excitement and anxiety-looking deep into his eyes with love and passion at his feelings.

'Is that a yes?!' asked Wilson curiously

'Wilson, I've seen your seriousness and read your mind and I trust that you are serious towards making this relationship and I cannot be a set back by continuing to pretend. You remember the night at the party? I found you very hot and cute and I was very happy seeing you looking at me with those romantic eyes but I was just too shy. You will never know how hard it is for a woman to see her prince charming and approach him-that's why I had to play those tricks for you to say the word which will spark our being together and here you are!' Wilson moved his head closer to her and kissed her and the gentleness of his kiss-triggered affections that navigated through their marrows and they accepted each other into a relationship.

Later that day, he went with her to a restaurant in town to have their dinner, they gave their order and the waiter brought it to them. As she was about to dip her fork into her plate of corn in front of her, our eyes met and she saw me with my son eating. She deliberately dropped her fork on the floor to call for my attention-and when I turned and looked at her, she pulled Wilson's head towards her and kissed him. I pretended not to see her doing that, and struggled to assist in feeding my son. I saw the mockery but calmed myself accepting the fact that I was married to a bad woman. When my son was through eating, I kissed him on his cheek and we walked out of the restaurant glancing at Rose as she sat and dined with her boyfriend. Rose noticed my glance and let out a hollow laugh to make me jealous.

When I left the restaurant, she bent her head to get a glimpse of me as I made my way to my carriage then she turned and looked at Wilson, coughed and cleared her throat;

'That was my ex-lover who just left the restaurant' she mentioned

'Is it? I guess he is now married because I saw him with a son' he replied stretching his neck to look again at me. 'Of course, he is married to one lady called Luna, well that was his choice and I guess they are living happily. Though, it does not concern me because I'm not part of him and I think if there is anything for us to discuss further, it should be about us.' she said smiling and holding his hand, and rubbing it softly.

'Look at you, what was that you did when we got into the restaurant- touching my ass?' asked Rose laughing as they make their way out of the restaurant to their carriage.

Two months later, Wilson visited her again at her invitation. She had prepared a delicious meal. Upon his arrival, she removed his jacket, hung it in her wardrobe and walked him straight to her dining table where they sat and ate what she had prepared. While they were eating, they spoke a great deal about themselves

'I must say I haven't eaten such tasty and delicious food ever since my parents died in an accident,' he commented supporting his head with his hand.

'You tried to tell me this at the club when we got interrupted by that nice music which drove us to the dance floor and we danced and went home so tired and we never spoke about it again. What happened to your parents?'

'On the eve of my eighteenth birth day, my mother and father were returning from a holiday trip in Dwarf land on, I was with my uncle. That night, a letter reached us about the death of my parents; I could not believe it until I saw their corpses, that was it. ' He turned and looked at Rose and said nothing again. Though the incident was history, Rose still felt sorry for his lost. He took it normally because it had past.

At night when they were asleep, the thought to be felt caught Wilson. He used his finger and romance Rose from her neck to her hips feeling and pressing her gently. She felt his hand and pressed on with thoughts ' maybe I should just give in to him lest I lose him for another repeating the mistake I made with Michael.' After serious contemplation, she turned and faced him exposing herself and they had sex, the excitement made him mad.

He later on proposed to her, and went and saw her parents. After a year, they got married, and the anxiety kept on until they got their first daughter. She was very happy especially as they watched over her as she played, ate and grew day by day. On a holiday to see the countryside, on coming carriages stopped abruptly, they were parading along the lane. Her husband pointed something on the road and she saw something else,

'Oh my God!' cried Rose running to the road

'What?' asked Wilson, wondering why she had screamed and was running to the road, she raised his head, stretched his toes and saw that all the carriages on the road had stopped hooting. Rose flipped spectacularly and carried the naked child on the road that happened to have caused all the carriages to stop and quickly crossed over to the pedestrian lane panting and carrying him onto her chest with a little smile. Wilson ran to her

'Which careless parent would allow their son down the road naked without assistance?' he asked angrily and they walked with the child towards the peacekeeping force's station to report. Luna's friend saw the crowd, walked in to find out what was the problem and saw Michael's son-Daniel in Rose's arm, and walked to her asking why she was with Daniel. When Rose explained what had happened to her, she took them to Michael's home. On arriving, they met me on the floor; they screamed and called me several times thinking I was dead, then they took me to the hospital when they realised I had some life in me. The doctors struggled and struggled to revive me until I regained consciousness. The first thing I asked after was my son. I love him so much. Rose gave Daniel to me and I held him close to my chest 'Can you remember anything that happened before you collapsed?' asked the doctor to get more information to add to my medical records.

'I was about dressing my little boy before I had a blackout and passed out and I don't remember anything till now,' I said it tiresomely and holding my head in pain, it seems I hit it when I fell on the floor.

'You need some rest' said the doctor adjusting my bed sheet to cover me. My son sat beside me holding and counting my fingers and I looked at him with tears rubbing his finger with mine.

Luna had not heard the news about my condition because she was busy having a nice time with Christopher drinking and drugging themselves. Her friend tried to reach her but she had already passed out. When she woke up the next morning, she got the news about my health and rushed to the hospital to check on me.

'I can't believe this, you are jobless, your husband makes sure you have enough money for your up-keep yet, the only thing you can do for him is neglect him and your son knowing his condition. What sort of woman are you? If I were you, I would rush my ass home and prepare something for them.' Luna's friend said to her in anger. Rose interrupted,

'What condition did I hear you speak of concerning Michael?' asked Rose

'Michael has cancer' she whispered in her ear. Rose opened her mouth wide, turned, and looked at Wilson. A pool of tears ran down her cheek in pity and she felt responsible.

'Maybe he knew and did not want to hurt me before separating with me,' she thought

Luna got to the hospital with the food she had prepared, and met me sleeping. She sat beside me and after three hours, I woke up and saw just the woman I never wanted to see at that painful moment. I closed my eyes and pretended to be asleep peeking from time to time until the doctor came into the ward to administer me medicine. After serious examination, the doctor saw me fit again to go home. After a week at the hospital, I was discharged from the hospital. Rose and her husband drove back to their home leaving us to ourselves. My parents were bitter when they heard everything, from time to time they kept on visiting me and when I had fully recovered, I hosted a party at my house thanking those who took part in the battle for my life. They were glad and happy that I survived it and cheered for my survival toasting their glasses of wine as we commenced the celebration.

'My name has been written in the book of death and I think the little I could do for my son while I am alive is to settle his future,' I thought, as I sat with my son in my arm chair on the porch in the warm summer gazing at nature,

'My boy, what would you like to become in the future?' I asked him in a concerned tone looking compassionately at him;

'A military doctor dad,' he replied innocently looking at his father with braveness taking his father's hand completely and pointing at a bird feeding on the crumbs at the garden.

'Father, why do you keep on repeating this same question time and again to me each time we sit to gaze at the beauty of our garden?' he asked, waiting curiously for his father's answer

'My son, you are just five and as you grow...get a seat and sit beside me and let me tell you why,' He rushed in to the house and carried a side stool and brought outside with him and sat beside me.

I began,

'I admire your brilliance my son but when you grow up, I want you to know that not all smiles that cross your path would be genuine and whatever thing you do in this world, do it with love and you should know this; your father might never be with you forever. I am terribly sick and someday you might lose me but that would not be the end of life, you will still have good people to take care of you like grandma and mum and the king' I pointed out.

'Where will you be dad?' he questioned innocently,

'With you' I replied. I was trying to prepare his mind but I realised how fragile his heart was and had to change the mains to keep him happy, Daniel climbed on my lap and sat on it leaning his head on my shoulder and said,

'Father, promise you will never leave me and go somewhere,'

'I promise' I said hoarsely wishing I had cleared my throat earlier before saying the word; I coughed and cleared my throat rubbing my hand on my son's head gently. 'I love you son,' I continued

'I love you too father' and continued

'Father why is it that mum doesn't spend time with us?'

'She will when she has the time. She's probably too busy chasing businesses to raise income for us'

The words of my son touched me but I swallowed the emotion to stop my son from seeing that something was wrong. When Luna returned home that same day in the evening, I engaged her in a query,

'Have you got a conscience?' I asked

'What's that supposed to mean?' she asked carelessly

'Everything… Do you realise you have a son who needs his mother beside him to comfort and care for him? Do you realise you have a husband in need to be loved and encouraged? All you do is gamble and flirt around... Yes, I know everything and I have warned you on several occasions but you remain adamant! Look let me warn you one more time, the road you are taking would lead you nowhere. Believe me and I would like to tell you this, should anything happen to me, you will not be the one to take care of my son, my parents will do that because I deem you unfit to do so, not with this form of recklessness in your altitude. If not for the dignity I want to maintain before my son, it would have cost me nothing to divorce you. But no, I wouldn't do that and I will still continue to give you a long rope to draw but remember, nothing lasts forever,' I said and left.

The sound of my anger triggered an emotional force that blew her compassion and affection from the depth of her heart to the exterior, and she understood my cry. I was really a man in need and she needed to spend time with me. She continued to date Christopher in secret but spent less time with him than before. What I needed was someone who would be able to take care of my son diligently when I was gone. I had doubts about my wife's capability. I went and paid a counsellor to help me counsel my wife with effort to changing her for good and in the event, she confessed her drug involvement. He reported it to me and we both counselled and advised her and took her to the hospital where she was checked into rehab.

One day, I sat weaving my basket. She walked to me and said,

'I love you Michael but I have done terrible things not worthy of your forgiveness. I am only a human and right now I feel so ashamed of myself' she said sobbing. I came close to her as she wept, drew closer to her and kissed her.

'I forgive you my love and your name has been rewritten in my heart, I myself cannot withstand the pain of leaving you people but everything happens for a reason,' I uttered slowly, calling on the little boy to join me in our reunion;

'My little boy, some day you will learn to understand why tears from your father always wash your hair,' I said to him rubbing my little boy's hair gently- smiling as my tears flew down my cheek. His mother looked at him and cuddled him too wiping his tears in misery and at the same time trying not to be so emotional. Daniel was just five and had the heart of his father, without him, I would have no reason to smile or live. He is the key and the hope of the family- the son of his father and the one to smile with before I journeyed to the land of the dead. Everyday seemed narrow and in the youngest of the day, I offered my prayer,

'My god, my god, as I leave for the land of no return, may your grace and love rest on my son as he grows to integrate in the world of misery and vicissitude, wherever he goes and wherever he lives, please be there for him –protecting and watching over him' I prayed.

I loved my son so much so that, there was no conversation I engaged myself in without mentioning his name and before he went to bed; I would sit beside him and tell him bedtime stories.

'A young boy from a polygamous home went to the stream to wash his clothes and as he squashed them on to the flat surfaced stone, he realised that, out of the twenty two pieces of clothes he took with him to the stream; he was able to wash twenty one. 'Where is the other one?' He asked himself aloud; 'I brought twenty-two dresses to this stream for washing and now I can only find twenty one- my mum would not be happy with me if I went home with only twenty-one.' he said disappointedly and dipped his hands into the stream searching for his dress. As desperate as he was, he began searching down the flow of the stream and as he marched in the direction of the water, he came across a woman with scabies all over her struggling to scratch her body on a palm tree. 'My son, my son' she called, he turned and gaze the woman. 'Please help me and scratch my back,' the old woman said. He went closer to her and scratched her back and when he had finished he asked her whether she had come across any piece of clothing floating down the stream.

' I saw it, it went rightward and if you follow quickly, you might get to it before it empties in to the river that might be too deep and swallow you,' she replied. He thanked her and continued running rightward as she had said waving at her as he rushed in that direction. A few minutes down, he saw an old man gathering his nuts and he asked, 'Father, father, have you seen any dress passing by the stream?' He replied, I saw the dress passing and by now it must have entered into the river, said the old man. Come and help me gather my nuts into my bush house.', he went without complaining and gathered the nuts with him quickly and escaped the gusty wind that was threatening to blow. The old man took him in his bush house. While in the house, he asked the young boy, 'My son, what are your wishes in this world?' The boy replied, 'To have a hut of my own and be rich,' 'So be it', the old man said smiling. 'Go in to the pot over there, he said pointing at his clay pot, 'and pick the egg that shouts –'leave me alone', and ignore the one which says take me.' He went in and did as the old man had said and picked just the one, which said 'leave me alone'. The old man gave him instructions on how to break the egg and waved at him as he went to his house.

When he arrived his home, he gathered all his family and bought a large piece of land. He had told them all that had happened and broke the egg - a beautiful hut appeared on his land with lots of money and carriages; he was very happy. His stepbrother got very jealous, picked some of his own dresses and went to the stream to wash them as his brother had done. He wilfully allowed his dress to be swept by the stream's current. He started searching for his dress; when he met the grandma, she begged him to scratch her back and he said to her; 'Do I look like your slave old woman? Show me the way to my dress if at all you saw it floating down the stream.' The old woman told him, it went rightward but you must hurry. He walked, and came across the old man who begged him to help him gather his nuts. He refused and asked if he had seen his dress. He said yes and added that it must be in the river by now. He then told him to go in and pick the egg, which said 'Leave me alone', and ignore the one, which said 'Pick me'. He went in the clay pot, and picked the one, which said 'Pick me' and returned home. When he gathered his family and broke his own egg in a land they bought for him, scorpions, snakes and all sorts of wild animals came out and killed him.'

When I finished, I turned and asked my son, which of the sons he would favour. I realised he had fallen asleep so I covered him properly with a loin, kissed him and left.

I went to my parlour, turned off all the burning candlelight, went into my room, met my wife and we slept. Luna was restless during sleep, something was troubling her; Christopher wanted her back in his life but she had categorically refused and he had threatened to come after her. She had made a mistake by telling him where she lived when they had their affair and Christopher was not willing to let go of her. He wanted her by all costs for them to play naughty games as usual. When she tried to sleep, the noise of the rustling tree branches would wake her up and she would shake in fright looking left and right as I dozed off. She fell into light sleep later and dozed off too.

Christopher came; he had had his usual dose of weed; he inserted his knife in its pouch and ran to our door. He was a man of tricks and had a universal key- he used it to open my main door and came into the house. The first room he went to was the room where Luna and I were sleeping. He dragged Luna towards him and her scream woke me up and as I tried to defend her, he pierced me on my chest and I fell over. The loud noise woke Daniel up and he came to our room for protection and found me lying in a pool of my own blood with a knife deep in my chest. He crawled to me calling me - 'father, father'.. He touched me and thought I was dead and as he raised his head up, he saw his mother being raped with a knife to her head and he watched her scream. My son picked up a bottle lying at the side of my bed and hit Christopher hard, he left my wife and punched my son most

117

forcefully, and he fell down and died. When the neighbours heard her screaming, they called the peacekeepers and they came and caught him while he was trying to run, got him well beaten and took him to the king. He was charged with rape and was beheaded in front of the people.

Every night before I went to sleep, I would walk to the ram pole in front of my house and pray for my son to be guided by the spirit of our ancestors. I never smiled with my wife like before. All I wanted was to see my son and hold him in my arms.

Luna went to Evelyn's house for visit; when she got in, she greeted her but she did not respond to her greetings but rather grumbled and gave her a bad look,

'I know everything about me disgusts you but I have come for us to talk. Where is your husband?' she asked confidently.

'He went out for a ride on his horse. I have nothing to say to you, you have ruined my son and killed my grandson because of your greed.' said Evelyn sobbing and wiping her eyes with her fingers.

'There is no need for tears, my husband has...' said Luna

'Correction, he is not your husband but your game boy' Evelyn interrupted rudely and looking at her thick red eyes, Luna pulled herself backward frightened at the way she looked then summoned courage from the depth of her heart and continued,

'Exactly what I am talking about, we have toyed with his emotions for too long and now I believe its time he knows the truth...'

'What truth?' she interrupted again

'The truth about his father... Look, I know how heartless you are but I just can't continue to carry this guilt in me. he has little time to live and all he needs is...'

'...love and care, not things that would tear his heart to pieces. Luna, my son is traumatised by his predicament, let us not ruin the few days he has left and send him to an early grave. Come closer to me' she called for Luna and placed her hand on her shoulder and continued,

'What you are trying to reveal would not only endanger my son but my husband as well. Do you picture yourself losing two of your loved ones at the same time, when the whole world knows about it? What integrity would I still have; to think that a mother ruined her son's life because of some nasty secret,' said Evelyn.

'I don't care about what you think, I love your son and I think he deserves better people around him. Each time I think of the way he pampered and advised me when I went wrong, I just can't hold my peace and I feel like all along I have been piercing his heart with a sword. Mother, do you really have any conscience at all? If you really do, then you would know that I am talking about your son, his right to know his true self.' she said weeping.

'My family would hate me forever; I wish I had told them the truth from the beginning. What should I...,'

Her husband came in from the back door and saw them crying,

'Did I miss something? What is going on? Is my son alright? he asked curiously,

'No!' they replied simultaneously,

'Then what's going on then?' he asked again

'It is not normal for two people to sit and cry without a reason. I heard your conversation, I was about to get in to the house before I heard you guys.' He said confidently eyeing them. Evelyn carried her hands on her head and later placed it on her mouth, then her waist, shivering in perspiration wondering what he would do to Luna.

'Evelyn, I have watched you for twenty nine years hoping that one day you will free yourself from the burdens you were carrying. Every night you slept with your burden, woke in the morning, and paraded with it. I kept on hoping patiently that one day you would share them...

'...What do you mean?' She asked in surprise

'I knew everything that took place. Though your son may be blank about it, I am not. I have my own secret that I've never told you; before I got married to you, I was the king of Brook's guard. As part of the code, all his guards were castrated to look huge and feel less sensitive to females. I was sent to kill one of his powerful traditional ministers and his entire family secretly because they were in possession of secret information. The king did not trust him and suspected he would have told his family about it after the first attempt of killing him failed. I was in that special squad to execute him. When I went to his home, I realised he had a three month old baby and for the first time in ten years of service, I felt emotional. I let them go, returned to the palace and told the king that they had escaped before I arrived. He was very angry and told me to leave him. I knew him very well; he had instructed my colleagues to eliminate me. I went in to hiding and immediately crossed the border and came into this kingdom to find refuge. When things had settled, I went back to Brooks and start staying inside the suburbs under a false name where no one would recognise me. I knew who I was but did not just want to let you know; that's why I went to the doctor and paid him to fabricate those stories you knew about me before now.

When you told me you were pregnant, I was happy, all that was pretence because right deep in me I was bubbling with anger knowing how unfaithful you had been. I traced you at some point before I really knew the whole story of

Michael and his brother and I became overwhelmed with your love for me to go to that extent.' They opened their mouths wide with shock and Evelyn spoke to him

'What sort of mystery man are you?' she asked

'Seriously' Luna added supporting her neck with her hands, amazed by his ability to contain his wife excesses but something remained questionable; would Evelyn's son forgive her for the emotional swagger that has ruined his entire life? Evelyn's husband turned and asked her,

'Now, have you finally made up your mind on telling your son who really his father is- in this his last few years before he joins his ancestors?

'Of course,' she replied uneasily flicking her eye balls rampantly in fright as they came to an agreement on disclosing the truth about Michael's parentage.

I was sitting in my house on a summer afternoon; they came with their heads hung low with shame as they marched into my house.

'My son, I have failed you in everything, I have not been a good mother to you. Please, I want to ask you to find a place in your heart to forgive me,' said Evelyn in a cold tone with so much guilt on her face.

I laughed in surprise,

'I do not understand what you are saying mum,'

'You were never adopted!' she said

'I'm still not clear, you told me that I'm from Brook's kingdom and that my parents were dead. You sang this like a song to me, every night and day, with us, and you advised me to call you mum and him dad! Is something wrong with you or are you hiding something from me?'

'Not really' father said gazing at his wife

'Your mother has been a wonderful wife and a wonderful mother too and though you know so much about her, there are things she failed to tell you. You know the law Michael; your mother had you out of wedlock and was scared for her life, that's why she had to cook all those stories to protect herself and you. Your junior brother's story is slightly different because, I was not able to father a child and she had to help me out. I am not the biological father of you both. Your mother had you before I got married to her, even your junior brother is not my son. You were at a tender age where you could easily accept anything and easily misinterpret them too. Today, we think it is your right to know who you are,'

'What are you talking about? Mum...'

'Yes, your father was right, many years ago when I realised your father was unable to father a child, I had to do something to have your brother. Kenneth Brook is the father of you and your brother...'

'...Kenneth Brook?!...that's Rose's father'

'Exactly-and the more reason why I took part in the separation of you both' she continued.

'What?' I asked in a loud tone rubbing my hand on my hair repeatedly and twisting my face in anger,

'I had to, I could not sit and watch you marry your sister; that's why I brought in Luna, and convinced her to have a child with you. When I noticed how deep in love you were with Rose, I had to put an end to it and so I encouraged her to marry you, which she did'. She said pointing at Luna as she shied away and hid behind her father -in –law.

I looked at my mother with so much hatred and said to her

'You are more than a beast mum; I regret having you as my mum. You have ruined my life. Why are you telling me all this now? You should never have, you and your husband are wicked and selfish,' I said glowering at them all, left the house, went outside banging the door harshly and made my way to my bench outside, crying. They could not understand, I wished I had separated with Rose before knowing her devilish and wicked plans!

Evelyn stood contemplating whether to follow me out or to stay in.

My junior brother was even more confused and could not believe it himself but that was the reality.

'How can my parents do this to me?' I thought and left the bench with a feeling of resentment, went in to the house and drove them all in anger.

'I know you are trying to kill me before I die,' I uttered as they left my house. Luna went with them and stayed with my parents for one week before reconciling with me, I had no choice than to accept their apologies. When I had accepted the truth about my parentage, we started making plans on how to get Kenneth Brook and Rose informed for me to integrate myself in to their family.

I rode with my horse into Rose's compound, knocked on the door and said my name.

'Why would Michael call me at this time of the night getting to midnight,' she asked herself as she woke up and opened the door,

'Hello!' she greeted.

'Hello, I know you are probably wondering why I called at this time of the night but I have something very serious and important to tell you,' I said grinning.

'Wow, you sound so happy. Have you heard any information exciting about your health, what is it about, could it be cured, who is the doctor...?' she questioned inquisitively waiting anxiously for a good response concerning her questions.

'...slow down Rose, it is about us...'

'Us?! There is no us Michael; you abandoned me for another and now you talk about us, sorry to disappoint you but I am happily married,' she replied angrily. Michael smiled again and it echoed in her ears,

'It is not funny Mic.'

'I know but you missed the point, I am your brother, sometimes things happen for a reason and in this case a good reason for a brother not to get married to the sister, I am the son your father does not know about and...'

'Are you ok Michael?' she asked; surprised to hear him speaking words which did not make sense to her. Michael knew she wouldn't understand and invited her over to his parent's place and left. When she came, my mother confirmed it to her.

'Michael is telling you the truth and it is a very serious issue,' Evelyn said soothingly. She went back home to her place on horse, told her husband about it and begged him to ride her to Michael's place. When she arrived and saw their seriousness, she informed her father in a letter. He did not want to say much so he invited all of them to his house. They planned to make the journey on Sunday, a day the family would all be home. They knocked and he went himself and opened the door and they went in to the house,

'Hello!' he greeted and showed them where to sit.

'What were you people trying to tell me in the letter?' Kenneth asked.

'Michael and his brother are your sons,' Evelyn uttered softly.

'I do not understand, how come?'

'Many years ago when we had....

'...yes, yes' he interrupted because he knew what he and Evelyn had shared

'ohhhhh! He exclaimed

'So you were on your fertile period?'

'Yes, 'she answered swiftly. He remembered Evelyn told him she wanted a son for her husband but he knew nothing about Michael because Evelyn left without telling him she was pregnant with Michael.

'My son, I could not resist the pain of childless families like your parents knowing that I could be of help to them, look how gorgeous you are,' he uttered in tears of joy embracing him.

'Thank you Michael and your family to think of me with this purity. Rose, it's nice of you to have brought your brother home and I'm glad you know each other this early and did not engage in an intimate relationship before discovering your connection' he continued.

In Rose's heart, there was a cloud of tears and agony, knowing that I was her brother. I had the feelings too but we all kept quiet, said nothing and did not change what they knew about us. Rose and I smiled looking at each other knowingly, and refrained from narrating our story. We embraced each other in happiness. Kenneth opened his cupboard, removed a bottle of wine and we opened it and drank in celebration. He had not heard the other side of the story and when we were drunk, he urged us to sleep in his house and avoid taking the risk of riding at night.

The next morning we woke up and the women went to the kitchen and made breakfast for the men. When we were at the table eating, I told them about my illness. They felt pity for me but to me it was ok and I had accepted the realities of what life had offered me.

After we had left to our various homes, my gentleness sparkled guilt in Luna and she couldn't bear living with me because she seeing me made things more painful. She went in, packed her bags and was about to leave the house when I met her.

'Do you really want to leave? I asked coldly and she sat down and wept. She couldn't look in to my eyes, tears ran down her cheeks with shame and the burden of her guilt was printed on her face.

'I can't stand you anymore, seeing you wallow everyday about our son keeps me in pain. I can never forgive myself for this mess but at the same time, I have changed and I want you to stop seeing me like the enemy.' She said bending her head down and supporting it with her hands. I came to her, cuddled her and wept with her.

'I have failed you and I have failed my son. Each time I sit, the memory of that night keeps on coming, I couldn't help myself, I couldn't protect my family and even as I was unconscious, I could hear my son and you screaming defencelessly in misery and agony. What else do you want me to do? There is nothing to think about other than my son. Is he really dead or is he alive somewhere in the invisible realms? He is somewhere outside there, defenceless and exposed to all sort of dangers. I am his father and was supposed to die and make places straight for him in the other world' said Michael

'I think of him too, let's get on slowly; losing two people at the same time hurts and I want you to know that your pain is my pain.' said Luna and we kissed each other in tears and I took her bags in to the room and arranged them in the wardrobe. Luna went upstairs and sat on the bed watching me as I unpacked her dresses. At one point; I stopped and became unstable,

'What Michael?'

'I'm having a blackout' I said and collapsed. Luna quickly called the neighbours and I was rushed to the hospital where the doctor examined me and saw the dangers and informed Luna about them. She absorbed the shock of the words, quickly cleaned her face with her tissues and pressed her emotions, then came to my ward and was looking after me with gentleness.

Rose came to me a few minutes later and whispered in my ears. She told me she had a child with me-a daughter. I could not believe myself. Just when I thought I had settled my problems, crisis was emerging. I felt paralysed and my fingers cold. I have committed the worst crime by having a daughter with my sister. It was hard to bear... we both cried but I was glad at some point because no one knew about it except us and she had given the child up for adoption before she got married, a secret we were not willing to let out.

Each time I closed my eyes, my son's image would appear in front of me and I would speak to him in my sleep without knowing the people around could hear me.

'I've failed you my son, and nature has failed to give me a second chance to correct my mistake. Keep this with you as you grow; my son, never leave your journey half-way until you reach your home and note that the road to home will be narrow and plagued with thorns, you yourself have seen how wicked the world is. Never stop dreaming; never stop hoping because I know you will be what you have always desired. Though the world has been graced with you, avoid making it your burden and walk in the path of truth and happiness...,' I was kind of hallucinating. My tone started going down and I turned and leaned on my right side. I could hear my wife pushing the nurse who was standing by her to do something. They alerted the doctor and I heard them say something but I was unconscious.

This is my story to the elders of our land. I know I've betrayed myself and I have betrayed my family but the world has to hear my story; damn the consequences because I know it is better to talk today for tomorrow's change. No one should ever suffer like me; no one should ever pass through my pain. I know I must die by man or by nature.'

When the village elders read his confession, they were amazed. It was not normal for a thing like that to happen for that long without the king knowing, especially with the numerous spies he had kept everywhere. They took his letter to the palace and handed it to Shaakhan who passed it on to the king and he read it,

'What, in my kingdom? Shaakhan,' the king called out aloud.

'Your Majesty,' Shaakhan replied running towards the king and bowing before him;

'Bring me the culprits,' said the king furiously with a dark frown on his face.

Shaakhan ordered twenty-nine warriors to follow him for the arrest of the culprit as the king had ordered. He knew he had confessed but the rest of his family did not. On a bright sunny morning, when the winds were so rich in moisture and places were just as wanted by the community for their traditional dances, Shaakhan came and stood at the village square where they were to perform their dances. That was their own way of socialising and making friends and women exposing themselves to their future husbands. Beautiful girls would tie their wrapper tightly round their loin in a systematic style and would show off their best dance moves to impress potential suitors. They gathered and just when they were about to commence their ceremony, Shaakhan and his men went into the crowd, arrested the culprit, took them into the dungeons and kept them there.

The king was to visit the four kingdoms to see the indigenes there. He was to be there for one week. When he returned, the first person to confront him was his daughter Josephine who saw how men were been dragged in to the dungeon by her husband.

'My father, the king, how many will you murder to fill your cup of cruelty? These people are your people and they deserves better. Who are you to them, their king or their enemy? When you came to the throne, look how happy they were, knowing that they were under your love and protection, but today they are muted and your laws are choking them but because they fear you, they aren't able to speak their mind. I'm speaking their mind not mine. My father, have compassion for your people and stop killing these innocent people of Duce who asked for nothing but care and mercy when they falter and to be loved by their king.' Said Josephine

'Very well spoken my daughter, one day you will succeed me and until then, you will never understand how difficult it is to wear the crown. Do you think I feel happy to see my children being murdered every day?'

'Leave us' the king said to his guards and they left closing the door behind them leaving only the king and his daughter to stand on the door with their spears crossed protecting any one from entering the ward.

'Before my father, our kingdom was enslaved by the four kingdoms. We were the smallest of them all; occupying a landmass a hundred times smaller than those of each of the four kingdoms. Our people were treated like slaves, with brutality. We paid taxes to them and they treated us like we were nobody; they ill-treated us, whipped us as we worked in their plantations and we only managed to have a meal a day to have little energy to continue working for them. Our cries were as useless as planting a plant at the heart of a desert and abandoning it to its own devices. My father was a man of myth and belief. He believed in the powers of the gods. One day, at midnight, when every worker had slept, he rose from his own hut, and went outside, taking with him an aluminium basin. He wounded his thumb with a knife and allowed the blood to drip into the basin. Then he took a white sheet, covered the top of the basin and somehow managed to enchant a series of words and the great god Krurice appeared from nowhere. He explained everything about how the natives and kings of the four kingdoms were tormenting the people of Duce. The god heard them and vowed to protect them only if he agreed to stain his hands with the blood of his people, which he did. He could not just kill anybody in the kingdom, thence he decided to kill the sick and some of the virgin in the Kingdom of Duce to protect the others. This is the side of history that no child of Duce knows about except we the royals and it is a secret we would never let the people know for them not to be scared of the future. Every market day, which was once a month, my father made sure he killed one person in the land of Duce who in one way or the other was involved in a crime. That was how he got to the throne, from their leader to their king. After two thousand years, the people of Duce were now able to be responsible for their own future. In the past, they were shown no mercy, when he had established the kingdom, he made it mandatory for the dying to make sacrifices for the living but it was not enough, we were still just independent after fighting a gruesome battle with the four kingdoms. Before I came to power, a prophecy came to me and my magicians explained it to me; how the land would cry out against me, I had to make the law even harsher if truly it was for the good of the people of Duce, what did the prophecy mean? If I killed more people in the land, their blood would cry out against me and you my daughter would give birth to a curse, because you are married to a person not different from me. And that curse would kill every lineage of the royal family including you, then a commoner would take over the throne of Duce, and would make the kingdom very powerful and all the laws that have hurt the indigenes would be changed and their future would be more certain. We have to sacrifice for the people of Duce if we want our children of the kingdom to exist free from the brutality of the four kingdoms. I've captured the four kingdoms by the blood of the people and by my blood the kingdom will be safe for eternity. This is a powerful secret and you must voice it to no one, not even your husband my trusted warrior because there will be Great War ahead between the cursed child and Kurice. Kurice would want not the royal lineage to be destroyed so that he can continue to feed on the blood of the innocent and so he will fight to kill our curses- the war is yet to come,' said the king, and Josephine understood the meaning of the killing and was frozen with fright. She uttered no word and went back to her own chamber. Tears ran down her cheeks and she cleaned it tightly with her hand so that no one in the palace could see of it. She had wanted to bear the risk and cheat on Shaakhan to have a commoner's blood that would be able to show compassion when on the throne but the king's word really meant something to her so she too must show her own love for the people of Duce.

They had captured the four kingdoms but for how long were they to suppress their powers and keep them under their feet? They knew how humiliating it was for the four kingdoms; a kingdom so big and great being captured by a kingdom so small, in comparison, like a dot on a piece of paper at war with the paper, history would always be reminding them about the way the head of their king was chopped off. These were the king's fears; he never wanted his people to go back to the days when they were badly treated.

He had to trade the strength of his kingdom by the blood of his people but did so wisely, with the criminals of the land. The people kept praying and wishing defaulters would have a say and be tried fairly in the palace court and if found guilty, they should be sent to prison, a place of isolation to make them realise what they did was wrong. For the king, their wishes were like yesterday and all he was doing was for the kingdom.

The next day, the sun was overhead, Shaakhan gathered the indigenes of the kingdom before the king and the king ordered him.

'Bring me the culprits' and he did and he gave him the royal sword, which Shaakhan used to cut through the necks of the culprits and their bodies were thrown in the burning furnace. Their heads were used to decorate the shrine of the god of war, and the god of war was pleased.

Chapter 9

Josephine had understood her father, what was she to do? She went up to Shaakhan in her fertile period and seduced him for him to make love with her. Shaakhan looked at her and smiled; this was one of his favourite moments and he doesn't play with it. He usually got annoyed when he sometimes asked for it and Josephine refused but today, she herself has initiated it. He first hugged her and held her close to him tightly rubbing his hands softly on her back with a strong affection. Then, he shifted her to his right side, using his left hand to unbutton his shirt and when he was through, he swiftly pulled it out of his body and laid her on their bed. He took his trouser off his body, quickly undressed her and they had a good time in bed with each other. It was fun and they had their pleasure like that continuously for a week before they started taking some days off. Finally, she became pregnant; she was very happy with the fact that she was pregnant carrying a child that held the destiny of the kingdom. At the same time as a woman, she was not happy with the type of child she was carrying- a curse that would in time end their lineage, not even the mother would be privileged to live. A child that would in time right the future for the people of Duce; to live happily, in peace and harmony with their neighbours, respecting each other's sovereignty and without fear of tomorrow. They wanted a kingdom free from attacks.

She invited her maids in her room. They fixed her hair, polished her shoes and dressed her in a fine cloth, and she was to appear before the king. When they had dressed her in her best garment, they walked her to the king. She was looked amazing and the king praised her, then, told her servants to leave them. She smiled and walked closer to the king,

'My lord, for thy wish of the kingdom is so desperately becoming visible,' said Josephine caressing her soft belly before her father.

'For sure, Josephine? The king asked, curiously eyeing her tummy,

'For sure my king,' she said and the king walked faster to her, embraced her and kissed her forehead. He was very happy; soon the kingdom would be void of doom. She had told her husband the night before she saw her father about her being pregnant and they had agreed on seeing the king two days before today when she revealed it to her father. It was not the excitement of motherhood, but the anxiety that the destiny of the kingdom would almost be secured. After all, it wouldn't stop her from appearing before her father the second time.

The day came when they were to appear before the king. She dressed beautifully as she did before and her husband was in his official wear. They came and stood before the king. Shaakhan stepped ahead of his wife, bowed before the king with his sword in front of him, and told the king they were expecting a child. He was happy and giggled vividly; he walked to them as if he was hearing it for his first time and embraced them,

'This calls for celebration; the princess of the land of Duce is with child.' said the king. The next day, he passed the message to the town criers to convey to the people of Duce. They were very happy when they heard and they walked to the palace on the day they were told and assembled there. The royal servants had arranged seats for them and they sat. The king then came before them, opened the ceremony and they commenced with the celebration. They drank and ate to their fill; when they were through, they left for their homes, and the king was pleased. Indeed, he had celebrated but his heart was still troubled, his lineage would be wiped out, something that was not easy for him or the rest of the royal families to bear. He loved his people but his love was silenced by his laws and was not felt by Duce people and so they were disgruntled. The king knew within himself that his people hated him but the royal secret had to be kept and so he kept on pledging his life and lineage for their sake. He loved them but he was their king and his emotions were not to be exposed in public. Moreover, his people wouldn't understand what he was going through for their sake. For two thousand years, their kingdom was under malicious attack by both the four kingdoms and the gods of the seas and mountains. If only you were in the mind of the king, then you would see that before he eats or swallows something, he has had thousands of thoughts about the future of his kingdom. The people didn't see it because the laws were tight and were still enslaving them like they had two thousand years before the king's father. These thoughts kept the throne burning and the king became restless.

After eight and a half months, the princess had reached her due date. They made it the most secret birth the family has ever had. They believed in what the magicians had told them about the princess delivering a curse and they knew not the way the child was to be like. Was the child to be a normal baby with great powers or a completely different child in an evil form to represent its mission to end the lineage of the king? The king had four families of magicians very loyal to him; the dwarf magicians, the temple magicians, the war magicians and the xenan magicians who fortified the king and told him what he needed to know about the kingdom. But this time, none of them was able to predict the sort of baby princess Josephine was carrying.

The dwarf magicians were in charge of relating themselves with the spirit of the ancestors and communicating their message to the king. The temple magicians were in charge of interacting with the spirit of nature. They used herbs and sometimes climbed up mountains to harvest herbs and would at times stay there for weeks or possibly months before climbing down with a bag full of herbs and whatever messages they had from the mountain spirits, they communicated to their king. The war magicians stood beside the king in invoking Krurice in time of war with the four kingdoms and contributed in fortifying the warriors going with them to and back on the frontline. Xenans were the last set of magicians but the most powerful; they were in charge of relating themselves with the demons and spirits of the air and communicating whatever message they had to the king. The king would then make his judgement from the messages he had received from them to be able to rule the kingdom.

Princess Josephine had seven days left to deliver the child of destiny. However, before that was to happen, the palace was already under attack by bad omen; it started first with the king's food, which suddenly turned bitter. He then summoned the royal chefs who cooked the food to explain why the food was bitter. They themselves were embarrassed, they've been cooking for the king for the past ten years; they could not understand it themselves because the food was always tested before being served to his majesty, the king. As the royal chef, they were very scared because any mistake to the king's food will mean losing their heads. One of them took the courage to taste the food himself before the king. It was very bitter indeed but that was something he couldn't say.

The king looked at him and saw him twisting his face as he struggled to swallow the particles of food he had scooped.

'How good was the food?' asked the king looking closely at them.

'Like aloe vera, the bitter medicinal herb my lord,' he replied.

The king ordered the palace guards to seize them and throw them in prison while an investigation was conducted. He invited the servants who served him and interrogated them but there seemed to be no answers to convince the king. He invited his magicians to see through and tell him the truth. They looked at the food and instead, saw beyond what the king saw; an omen, a perception that Krurice was suspecting something fishy. They told the king it something far from a mere error in the preparation of food. It wouldn't take long after the king was told why the delicious meal went bitter before the god would visit. The king was walking into his chamber when lightning struck and a heavy rain began to pour. A flash of light shone through into the palace and slid through the king's garment and tore it into two pieces, which fell apart rendering the king naked. A chunk of dust appeared and spun around violently through every object it came in contact with and absorbing it to itself forming a large tornado in front of the king at his palace. Then Krurice fully appeared in his true god form. His limbs were twice as long as that of humans and ended in claws. His legs very hairy and shaped like those of a donkey, erect with a human body and a head like that of a dragon, his eyes burning red this time around. Then he spoke to the king;

'What have I done, why do you want to deny me of what is mine - the blood of your people. For fifty years, I've served as a guard to the kingdom of Duce seeing them through wars with the four kingdoms and just in your years of reigning alone, I've submerged the four kingdoms under your rules with my powers and you want to pay me back by ending your lineage, breaking the oath your father took with me? I do not ask for much, only for me to use the blood to keep me alive and healthy and my magic fit and active to be able to defend the kingdom. I have not come here to harm you but if you want, I will. You must kill the princess and spill her blood over my shrine and I will consider nothing ever happened and would continue to serve the kingdom under the pact and oath I had with your father, just like I have done in the past years.' said Krurice with a large and thick voice and a flammable breath he exhaled. The king was confused and he stood gazing at the god Krurice. The families of magicians quickly sensed the trouble the king was in and appeared in the chamber of the princess, and surrounded her in circle holding firm their wand to retaliate any attempt to kill the princess. Krurice disappeared and pretended to have gone to his shrine. The magicians left quickly to the king and instructed the guards to walk out. They then tore the door blind, covered the king with it, took him to his chamber and dressed him. The king was in shock, unable to speak to anyone with his eyes wide open and rolling from one end to the other. The guards had been instructed to tell no one, not even the king's wives who were resting in their quarters weaving their threads and humming their traditional songs blessing the day for its gentleness, not knowing what had happened. The head of the temple magicians dipped his hand in his sack and removed from it a chopped stem of a greenish soft of a palm tree, and folded it and placed it on the king's mouth. In addition, he forced a bottle of herbal concoction into the king's mouth for him to drink. They struggled and when he drank it, they rested him on his bed to face the ceiling and stood closer to him chanting and praying to the spirits to save the king. Josephine herself was unable to understand what was going on, she walked to the king's chamber to find out from her father and met the magicians who had crowded her father and the room full of smells of burning charms to scare away any evil spirit coming near the king. She was denied access into the king's chamber so she returned to her chamber and was restless peeping through windows to see if she could see anyone to talk to.

Krurice slid through the princess's door as a fine water mirage and was just about to blow out a spell, which could've killed the princess when the war magicians appeared in the princess' chamber and seized her. They took her into the underground chamber of the palace and spelled it with powerful magic tough for Krurice to quickly break through. Krurice was not happy and returned back to his shrine resenting both the king and the magicians and declared war on the magicians, to be able to kill the princess. Behind closed doors, the four kingdoms have begun forming alliances with each other to wage a war against the Duce kingdom in an effort to regain their pride and status, they couldn't bear the shame of seeing a small kingdom vetoing over them, making their people pay taxes to them. In their tunnels and forests, they began training warriors secretly without the knowledge of the king of Duce or the commanders he appointed amongst the four kingdoms. They were very clever and did their training only at night when every human and animals in the land had gone to sleep and the next morning, they would be very exhausted and you could easily notice from the way their eyes were drooping but no ordinary civilian could understand.

Four hours later, the king rose and saw the magicians; he wasn't sure if he had actually missed something and he didn't want to ask any of them. He turned behind him and gripped his sword, the magicians bowed and he stood up and walked from one end to the other looking into their eyes as he passed each of them. There was still no volunteer to explain what had happened. Though he could recall past events right up to the point when Krurice spoke to him, the rest was a mystery. He himself did not realise he was naked before the arrival of the magicians. He turned and faced them and saw on their faces how eager their minds were to say something to him. He raked his hands through his hair and asked,

'Were you all able to meet Krurice or did he go before you all came?' he asked his magicians technically prompting them to say something more than just seeing Krurice and fortunately, they opened up and told him everything and he said to them,

'Tell no one,' said the king

'Yes sir,' the magicians replied

Amongst the royal families, only the king, Princess Josephine and the magicians felt the tension and knew the fate of the kingdom. The king became more scared, the pressure was unbearable; the people of Duce kept urging and revolting against the king to stop sacrificing the blood of humans. They were doing so for the sake of their loved ones, friends and families who kept on losing their lives. The king was fighting with the gods to die and not live to end the pact of blood and oath that led to human sacrifices in the land of Duce.

On the last day of the seventh day left for the princess to have the baby, the king and the magicians went down to the underground chamber and watched the princess deliver. The royal midwives did not have access and the magicians were the ones to assist the princess, Shaakhan was still in the Brook kingdom carrying on with his duty. As the clock hit 6:00 in the evening, she gave birth. The child was very normal in physiology like humans, far from the beast the king had suspected, but he had blue eyes something, which seemed a nightmare to the king. Each time he cries, his eyes glow reflecting the blueness of his eyes. The magicians bowed together with the king and they dressed the child and kept the child in the palace. They refused to show the people the child born by the princess. Shaakhan was informed. When he heard about his wife's delivery, he got into his carriage and came back to the land of Duce to see his child. He was filled with great joy and carried his baby in his arms, lifting him very high above his height before giving him back to his wife.

Every day, every time the princess was to breast feed the child, tears flew down her cheeks on to the eyes of the baby. They had named him Zalinda Khlin meaning-kingdom's destiny. As his eyes would glow, she herself was afraid because she had given birth to a child that would in time end their lineage though they knew not how but the prophesy had said soon.

"A child born of the most powerful warrior of Duce in companion with the princess would end the lineage of the king, freeing the people of Duce from human sacrifices."

Zalinda Khlin shocked the mother when he was three months old. One day, when she sat on her bed feeding him, and the drop of tears from her cheek fell on his eyes again, Zalinda Khlin raised his hand, wipes his mother's tears and asked,

'Mama, why do you always cry?' her hair stood straight in fright and her adrenalin rose, she threw him on the bed and screamed.

'He has started, he has started' she screamed, running to the king. The king asked her what was wrong and she told him what happened. He sent his guards to call the magicians from their temples. They came in a rush and stood before the

141

king bowing to the ground. The king told them what the princess had said, and they all walked in to the princess's room and they met Zalinda Khlin playing with things.

It seemed as if nothing had happened and he was on the bed sucking his finger and wriggling with excitement. Seeing the child, the magicians suspected something but kept it to themselves, they already knew his mission even long before he was born - to end the king's lineage. The princess herself was now scared of even carrying the child. Each time she was to feed him, she always made sure she was in the midst of the magicians.

The king loved hunting, and from time to time, he went in the forest to hunt. One day in the forest with his guards and servant, he saw Zalinda Khlin creep past beside him. No one else saw him except the king. Even though he tapped his nearest guards to look towards the place where he saw him, they did not see him. It appeared strange to him, he kept on tapping their shoulders and pointing at the direction in which Zalinda Khlin was creeping but no one seemed to be seeing what he was seeing. The guards became scared of what was happening to the king; they carried him, sat him in his carriage, and took him back to the palace. They explained all that took place in the bush to the magicians, they burned another charm in front of their king, the charm was so powerful that Zalinda Khlin sneezed heavily and Krurice shook.

'The child is born' said Krurice and continued.

'They have not heeded my word, I'll make the king a laughing stock by the people of this kingdom and far away. This kingdom was nothing without me,' said Krurice with burning anger and he left his shrine and raided the palace. The magicians stood firm with their wands when they sensed his coming, Krurice blew fire mixed with magic, and killed four of the king's magicians. The war magicians took the princess and the child, Zalinda Khlin and disappeared with them to the kingdom of Brook. Krurice searched through the palace and saw no sign of them, he started hunting the common people of Duce, killing and feeding on them and when his belly was full, he went and rested in his shrine. While in his shrine, he called the king's name three times, placed a bowl of water in front of him, and conjured a white magic powder in to his palms. It appeared within the blink of an eye, he sprinkled some on to the water and called the king's name three times again, this time adding some magic portions of his pre-enchanted herbal concoction on to the water and commanded the king to appear before him. The king was sitting on his throne surrounded by his magicians, then of a sudden, his soul began to leave him heading towards the shrine of Krurice. The head of all the king's magicians, Papurose Zuroru, felt the king was not in himself, his eyes were stiff and his body stiff, but he had not yet noticed that the king's soul had left him heading to the shrine of Krurice. He first walked closer to the king and touched him with his staff but there appeared to be no response. He now turned to inform the other magicians, and saw the king's soul dissolving through the palace walls heading for the shrine. He disappeared and stood well ahead of him and punched the air forward with his hand releasing his magic onto the king and sending his soul back to his body. When his soul had gotten into his body, the king shook as if he was just from sleep. Krurice had wanted him to appear before him for him to be able to instil into his mind one of his most wicked and dangerous demons to be able to cast out the love he has for his people. The war magicians and the princess and child had arrived the Brook kingdom; the people of Brook under the command of Maxan were planning to attack

Shaakhan's home and kill him. He knew not and the magicians had not seen it in their screening. He was back from work and saw the princess,

'What are you doing here my princess?' he asked with surprise on his face seeing them, they had not told him they were coming.

'Fleeing away from the god's anger, Krurice wants to kill our blessed baby,' said the princess.

'Krurice! Why, or has it asked yet again for another sacrifice?'

'No, my love, I do not know why he seek to kill our child, but all I want is to see our baby safe, away from the monster of a god.'

'Very well, you made the right decision,' said Shaakhan, he then took the baby from the princess and rested him on to his chest. At eleven o'clock when they were asleep, the secret Brook warriors attacked Shaakhan's home with their sword, spears and arrows striking and destroying everything that stood on their way. Shaakhan had just gone to bed and heard the clinking of objects as the warriors were making their way to his room. He shook and woke up getting his wife up as well and they bent their heads down below their beds raising it up gently to see what was happening, the moon was shining and its light very bright, Shaakhan jumped and blew off the candle light beside his bed and went back and positioned himself. The warriors walked past from one room to the other, he saw shadows and crept to the basement where his weapons were and gripped his sword. He turned and told his wife, to go for the child. He himself went straight to the direction of the warriors and engaged them in a fight, which was fierce and gruesome. He slaughtered hundreds and wounded hundreds but they were just too much for him to keep fighting, his energy was running out, they started getting part of his body and cutting deep with their swords. He succeeded in taking them out of the house to a more opened field, but they wouldn't allow him to get a space to roar for the other warriors in their camps to come to his aid and they kept on slicing him from any part of his body their sword could touched. He was losing lots of blood oozing from his body like a fountain, then they soon heard a cry- a sound of a baby. They thought and remembered how Shaakhan had raided their kingdom, killing women, children and their warriors. Some of the warriors left to check inside Shaakhan's house, the princess went under the bed with the child and pressed him tightly to her chest so that even if he cries, the noise wouldn't be heard. They walked up to Shaakhan's bedroom and found no one. They turned to walk out when the baby struggled and made a soft noise; they searched the house cutting through everything they were able to lay hands on. Then came from under the bed the princess of Duce kingdom, what a sweet moment for them as they burst out knowing they would kill them all and send their heads to the king of Duce telling him about their revenge.

Sadly for them, it wouldn't be what they were hoping. Zalinda Khlin twisted his body and slid from his mother's hand and fell to the ground- transforming into a full-grown human, his eyes burning and glowing bright green. The power of his magic was released and it caused confusion amongst them and they started fighting each other and killing themselves. When they were all dead, he retransformed into a child. The princess was frightened and ran outside and screamed, it was then that the other warriors in the camp, two miles away heard and armed themselves and came to see what was going on in Shaakhan's home and met him badly injured, they took him and commenced treatment of his wounds.

It wasn't clear to the princess for a child whose destiny was to end the lineage of the king and human sacrifices to protect the very people he was destined to kill. She got in to her carriage with her baby and husband and they rode to Duce. When they arrived Shaakhan explained everything to the king as he had seen it happened. The king ordered for him to be taken care of in his chamber and told him to have enough rest, but the king had not heard the odd part of the story, she told his father and added;

'I do not understand why he turned to protect us,' said the princess, the king nodded, 'Huh?!' and he himself was confused. He said nothing, he could hardly think why the child could have done that, they were not surprised about the magic he was having but the various circumstances under which he used it remained a puzzle to them. The king sat back on his seat exuding the mysteries of Zalinda Khlin.

Chapter 10

A year later, Krurice realised how serious the king was in changing the situation for his people. The king had reformed the laws; criminals were now sent to prison and virgins were no longer sacrificed, Duce indigenes were at peak of happiness glorifying their king. The sadness of their yesteryears was gradually being forgotten.

The king was under pressure from the god Krurice whose powers depended on the blood of humans- the virgins of the kingdom of Duce. For the first time in fifty years the people of Duce saw a brave king, to them it was the beginning of good times. To Krurice, it was a mockery. For fifty years, he had stood by the kingdom and now, they have decided to starve him. He was creased with anger; he took one of his chalices of blood, went to the king's palace, killed one of the king's wives and sucked her blood into the chalice using his magic, then went back to his shrine and placed the cup before him. He stretched forth his hand and his wand appeared on it. He then pointed it to the chalice spinning it softly in the open air. A flash of light appeared from nowhere and beamed on the surface of the cup. A billow of smoke rose from the chalice up to the heavens and Krurice followed the path in which it rose by raising his head, at a height of eight feet. He used his wand and waved it through the smoke invoking all the dead in both the Duce kingdom and the four other kingdoms.

Lightning struck, thunder rumbled and a torrential rain fell across the kingdoms. From their graves, the dead rose with rotten bodies and no heads. He enchanted them and the dead went about in the kingdoms, killing any human they met. The people of Duce were frightened by it and they called them Canapians; they raided the land killing and killing, no one was safe and they flew in to the valleys to take cover.

One of the indigenes ran, stumbling on the hills and valleys to the palace, panting heavily.

'My king, my king' he called out,

The king ran to him,

'Speak, for what troubles you troubles me,' said the king curiously

'Misery, misery, the land is under attack by the canapians, they are raiding the land killing in numbers...'

'Canapians?!

At once, the king ordered his warriors to defend the masses, and they gripped their swords and arrows and went on the front line to war with the dead. Tension grew in the palace, the magicians were under pressure to do something to save the land, they were injured and the dead were filling the king's courts.

'Is this the end?' asked the king, it was like waking up from a troubled sleep and receiving a sudden smack on your cheek with everybody yelling at you. His kingdom had never been faced with such raid from the canapians, though they have heard stories told as tales of something of a sort that took place some three hundred years ago.

'Is it the rage of the gods or revenge for the king's disobedience?' the people thought.

Shaakhan, the king's favourite warrior had just recovered from his injuries in an attack by the four kingdoms secret warriors to regain their land. Actually, their god, the protector of their land had cursed them inflicting pain they would never in their history forget; their dead were resurrecting and preying on humans, sucking their blood and releasing them to their master Krurice which he used to boost his powers. The canapians from the four kingdoms were preying on the indigenes, heading towards Duce with the warriors aligned fighting to death to save the people and the kingdom. The rate at which people were killed by the canapians became alarming; even the moon was frightened and hid behind the earth preventing its rays from reaching below. Everywhere was dead silent, the birds hid in their nests and all the animals escaped to their habitats.

Zalinda Khlin was asleep and was in his tenth month. He shook and opened his eyes and the first person he saw was his mother with her hands tight and shaking with fear. He went down from his cradle and crept to the window looking outside. There appeared to be no sign of any body, they were either in their huts, homes or had escaped somewhere in the palace, across to a distance. He saw a group of people walking slowly towards the palace, half flesh half skeleton and even the areas covered with flesh had decayed partially. He froze and became stiff, like a statue. Then he commanded his soul through an enchantment and his soul left him, and ran with a speed of seventy-five miles per hour reaching near the canapians. He saw them for himself,

'They're cursed creatures, the work of magic,' he thought. He was invisible such that even the canapians could not see him. He meditated and his eyes burned yellow, he raised his hands up and a sword appeared immediately. He raised it above and was about to strike through the first canapians when his mother came calling,

'Zalinda, Zalinda,' wondering where he was, and searching for him in the palace. He knew if his mother saw him in that stiff form, she would be scared and would displace him, which would make re-entry of his into his body difficult. He dropped the sword and ran back in with the same speed he used before and commanded his soul to fit into his body. It thus fit in time before his mother could discover he was beside the window.

'There he is, common baby, you got me scared,' said the princess and she lifted him up to her chest taking him into her chamber to clean him up. Outside the palace stood the magicians, sweating and panting, searching within themselves the last of their powers to join forces and fight the canapians. The king called his servants, and they dressed him up in to his warrior's dress. He adjusted his helmet, picked up his sword and fitted it in its sheath tied around his loin. Then, he held his armour firm and said to his family,

'I'm going out to defend the people of the Kingdom of Duce from the wrath of the canapians caused by my own hands.'

'Father, be careful,' said the princess. They all stood watching the king as he walked out of the palace. At once, his warriors marched behind him and he led them to battle with the canapians. When Shaakhan heard that the king was at the frontline fighting, he retreated with his own warriors and they headed north towards Cungham to meet the king and support him. Shockingly for them, the canapians were killing the warriors but when they got to the king, they passed and left him untouched. He himself was surprised, before leaving the palace he thought maybe it was time for the prophecy to be visible and all those who knew the prophesy thought so too. 'What is happening?' the king thought. From behind him came a large bellowing, the warriors retreated, pointing at the source. The king turned swiftly and cut through the air with his sword trying to reach the very flesh of whatever was behind him, raising his head, he saw;

'Krurice?!' The king called out in fright, opening his eyes wide, gazing at the god of war. He was not sure if he was seeing him or imagining him and he tapped one of his warriors,

'Yes my lord,' he responded.

'Are you seeing what I'm seeing?' asked the king.

'Yes my lord, the god of war,' he replied

'Really! Really,' the king continued. Then Krurice laughed out with a loud voice like a thunder striking a tree and stopped abruptly. Then pointing, at the king he said,

'You ungrateful king of Duce, you have refused to heed my word and your obstinate nature has brought massive death to your people. I have cursed the land for you to see that whatever the gods want, they always have. You are just a mortal and you do not know the pain faced by the god to protect you and your kingdom, far be it for you to now treat me your god like an outcast.' said Krurice

'What do you want god of war?' asked the king.

'I forbid you to ask me such a question again. If there is anything I want, it is the life of your grandson Zalinda,' replied the god of war. Krurice walked closer to the king, the king shifted backward, and the warriors stood panicking. He vomited fire and killed a thousand of the warriors, then seized the king and disappeared with him in to his shrine. The magicians saw that; the spirits of the earth were silent, they broke their staffs, buried it in the earth and meditated, crying and using their magic trying to subdue the powers of the canapians. One hundred nights and days came and passed and their king was nowhere to be found. The news of his kidnapping by Krurice had reached the palace and they stood weeping for their king. Maybe it was over and the anger of the god of war was headed straight to the palace to get hold of Zalinda. The eyes of every one were red with tears.

Back at the shrine, Krurice conjured his goblet that appeared at his right hand. He sprinkled some portions of his pre-enchanted white powder onto the goblet, then added some saliva in it and enchanted pointing his hand to the cup. A billow of smoke rose from the cup in fine molecules of flashed lights popping as it moved upward. He used his wand and directed the spell to the king and the spell transformed the king into an antelope, he smiled and said to himself,

'I have preserved the king and he will remain untouchable for as long as he lives. The kingdom owed it to me to keep on sacrificing to me their god.' He turned and gazed at the king in his uncomfortable shape and smiled and named him Kingtelope. He then added another spell onto the Kingtelope so that anyone who saw him would love him rather than harm him. Then, he sent him away into the bush. At night, he went and stood at the palace gate weeping and when the morning was nigh, he jumped back into the bush, amongst his fellow antelope. He was very quiet and worried. When they went to find food for themselves, he always stayed back rankling at his woes.

One night, he came again and stood at the palace gate. The magicians were opposite the palace enchanting; they had drawn a magical circle and stood on it. Then, an omen breeze blew and their circle went up in flames. They turned and saw the Kingtelope, his body glowed and his furs rippled and flushed on to them a powerful charm, which was coming to them with absolute force. They used the wands they held with them and stopped the charm reflecting it back to the Kingtelope. He cried out and they heard from his voice a troubled mystic sound, like that of an owl, which awed them. At once, they chased the Kingtelope and he ran into the bush. They returned back, and went inside the palace. The next day same time, they hid beside the palace, hoping the Kingtelope would show up. They waited and waited and just when they were about to go back to the palace; the

Kingtelope turned up, reflecting the same charm as he did before. They suspected it to be their king but they were not sure. They used their wands, conjured a net, controlled it with their powers on to the Kingtelope, and caught it. The temple magician removed from inside their sack a strong herb mixed with the mandrake roots and chafed the entire body of the Kingtelope.

'Wow!' they exclaimed as the king came whole and naked. They quickly covered him with cloths and took him to his chambers. He was confused and unable to talk; his transformation sent him to a state of confusion and he shivered as he lay on his bed. His wives came to him cuddling and rubbing their bosoms on his hand, this was to show they cared and had missed the king. They sat close to him, monitoring him. When the king was better, he showed himself to his people and they were very happy. They thought he was dead. The king looked at them and they saw in him a true contrition. It was far too late for him to show this type of feelings; their people were dying in the hands of the canapians, a blood-sucking creature. They knew not where it was from though the warriors and the king together with the magicians had an idea. The entire population was kept in the dark, far from predicting that their lives were in danger because the king wanted to save his grandson.

Back in the palace, the king turned to the magicians,

'How much time do I have left to die with my entire family?' asked the king in a perturbed tone roving around the palace, then he rest his hand on one of the magicians' shoulder,

He answered,

'My lord, many more years, what is happening now was unrevealed to us and we couldn't have predicted it, but in my opinion, the raid of the canapians are the doings of the god of war, there are no doubts and our problem should be how to tackle the god and give in to his demands,'

'Demands?!' he shouted, the king looked at him intensely and asked.

'Are you for the god or for the people?'

'For the people; if we agree to take Zalinda for sacrifice, the god Krurice would be blinded by happiness and would think we really are going to sacrifice your grandson. I know a spell to reverse the spell Krurice had been using to control the dead. I can then send them back to their graves to rest; my fellow magicians would seize the child. If by any means he gets hold of him, the anger of failure would frustrate the god of war and we could from there to try to attack the god with our powers.'

'Very well spoken, I will think about it and give you my words tomorrow,' said the king.

That night, the king could not sleep, in bed in thoughts about the prejudice of his kingdom which he alluded to his father for being the cause of the curses raiding the land. Had it been he had not gotten into an oath with the god of war, his kingdom wouldn't have been in calamity, his struggles to change things and set his people free has only strained his relationship with the gods.

'Maybe I went the wrong way, maybe I choose the wrong time or the faith of my people is not strong enough to split this coalition between man and god. I feel for them, I feel for our losses and I wished the gods could feel the same, knowing all we want is another way of pleasing them rather than the sacrifices of our beloved ones. One man, one life in the mirage of obscured realities,' the king said to himself aloud while in his chamber in bed rolling from one end of the bed to the other, pissed off by the thick loin that slid off the bed and fell on the ground. In agony, he screeched hysterically. The guards quickly ran into his chamber to know what was wrong with their king, and met him still troubled and worried.

'My lord, is everything alright?' they questioned darting from end to end to make sure he was not under the attack of the canapians. When they were convinced he was not under attack, they stood straight with their left hands behind them and the right hand holding their spears looking at the king. He ordered them to stand outside, he himself didn't realise he made such a loud noise to attract his guards. When the guards left, he woke up from his bed and sat in his traditional armchair that stood beside his bed with his bush-lamp. He turned the wick of the lamp up to increase the brightness, walked and stood by his window gazing at the outside. His eyes went across the palace and he saw from afar the canapians standing still like a crowd of statues waiting to murder any human that would cross their path. He took a deep breath, turned and looked at his room once more and back at the canapians again. His warriors were at a distance - aligned to defend the masses but not too close. He knew he was a powerful king that's why his people were devoted to him. He was not willing to abandon them in time of need. He ordered for the magicians at once to appear before him,

'Let's give it a go,' said the king

'Yes my lord,' they replied and left the palace at once. They rallied outside the palace with all their magical equipment and potions. At once, they sent for the princess to bring the child. They cut their thumbs with their daggers and one after the other, they held their thumbs above their magical chalice and blood oozed from their thumbs in to the chalice. The head of the magicians took the chalice and raised it high above hurling it north, south, east and west. Another magician then drew a magical circle on the ground that encircled all of them. The one holding the chalice placed the chalice at the centre and they all held their wands pointing at it in silence meditating within themselves. After thirty minutes, they removed their various magical potions from their bags, drank and spat some on to the chalice. Zalinda was then brought to them; they held him up high and underwent a four-minute incantation before lowering him down. The powerful spells from the north, south, east and west flew on to him in fine dust particles entering through every pore he had on his body. After it was over, they gave him the blood in the chalice and he drank of it. When they were through with the rituals, they went with him inside the palace. The king held his grandson, kissed him and cuddled him. He knew anything could happen that could result his son losing his life, something that was hard for him to bear. When the morning was nigh, he announced to the people of Duce,

'By this time tomorrow, the prince Zalinda will be sacrificed to Krurice to end the rage of the gods and bloodshed.'

He said so because he did not know if the prince would survive the powers of the god Krurice. It was not as if he lacked trust in his magicians but he knew the powers of the god. Even the magicians feared him and knew that what they were going for was a gamble though he hoped something good came out of it. No one had ever dared to tease the gods in the way he had and he himself had seen the wrath of the god. He kept this behind him and stretched his body on and on to reduce his tension.

The next day, the king mustered his warriors, and stood in their midst with his family and the magicians stood in front and at the back with their charms and magical equipment. They then commenced the march to the shrine of Krurice.

The women, children and men of the kingdom gathered, stretching their hands to touch Zalinda for their last time before he was to be sacrificed, crying and waving their hands as he passed where they stood. His grandson he had gushed over with pride was now victim of a gamble, a game they were not sure would succeed.

When they arrived the shrine, the magicians removed their gneisses from somewhere in their sacks, built an altar, and laid Zalinda on it. They performed another ritual invoking Krurice. From within the god came a stream of smiles. It gladdened his heart to see the king's grandson being brought before him. He was still invincible and like he normally does, he spun the dust violently and appeared before them. Zalinda's eyes glowed immediately, his magic charged up. At once, the sun ceased to beam, he stretched his hand forward and the glow from his eyes took Krurice adrift - far away in to the dark air. He then lurched his head forward with his eyes focused, fluttering him about to his satisfaction with his magic which jabbed every part of his being before he slammed him to the earth. At the same time, Krurice retaliated, wove and flushed his own spell, it was very powerful and it hurled Zalinda far away. He hit his head against the tree so violently that his skull would have split if not for the magic he used to repel himself from the oak tree to feel less impact. He stretched forth his hand towards krurice, releasing a punching spell that hurled Krurice faraway, transforming him into a hard cuboid. The magicians stood watching the drama with their wands tightly held in their hands. The king and his family were amazed by the powers possessed by Zalinda.

'The prophecy never said anything about this!' said the princess.

The warriors' squeaked then caught themselves and forcefully swallowed their saliva numbing as they watched the child display.

Frustrated by the princess' kid - Zalinda, Krurice woke up from the shabby dust chunk Zalinda had thrown him squawking with anger. Zalinda marched and stood in front of him triumphantly. It was unusual for him being challenged by Zalinda whom he had thought was a mere child. He mustered some strength and took on his godlike form then watched Zalinda for a few minutes as he crouched ready to defend himself. Krurice shook with despair for his miscue. Numbed by the greatness of the powers in Zalinda, he turned and asked the king.

'Is it again another tease?' he uttered hoarsely standing firmly, wanting to smack the king with his powers. The magicians raised their wands towards him, he saw their readiness and like a spiral wind, he faded out of their midst. The warriors of Duce were left dead cold, frozen by the powerful magic used on Krurice, which scared him away. They began rambling in their minds whether to call him god or just merely the king's grandson. As they stood contemplating, rain fell from the sky on to them, followed by heavy thunder, which was accompanied by lightning. A voice whispered somewhere in the dark, the fear numbed them and as though nothing had happened, the first ray of the sun glowed, touching the crust of the earth before the whole sun appeared. Zalinda licked the drops of rain that had settled on his upper lips gazing at the sky aimlessly. Then, he turned and looked at them all and smiled leaping there and there; the magicians lowered their wands and came closer to him. They knew at this time that his anger had been suppressed vehemently, and one by one, they embraced him. The king was the last to give his embrace, he had only heard about his powers but had not seen, not until he saw for himself the magic in Zalinda. When they took him back to the palace, the people were confused.

'We thought the king said Zalinda was to be sacrificed to the god Krurice?' said some group of comrades in the crowd

'Maybe the gods have rejected him,' another group continued as if they had heard the doubts of the first comrade.

Zalinda was given a bath and laid to sleep in his cradle. His mother kept on gazing at him, with that gaze, the look so charming of a lovely mother to her child. he too gazed at her as his soft eyelids weakened to sleep, in trust and in his mother's arm.

Chapter 11

The next morning, when all had been forgotten about the canapians, they came in their numbers invading the land with massive rage. The god Krurice had woven a more powerful spell to enforce their rage, and they were killing indiscriminately. Everywhere everyone went to in the kingdom were splashes of blood on rock surfaces. Again, another realm of confusion had been instilled in them and the pressure to save the land was now on the rise. Shaakhan gathered his warriors to the frontline cutting through every canapian. However, their cuts were just a delay because they were indestructible and each of their cuts healed instantly before their very own eyes. The warriors saw that the canapians had grown more powerful than before and under their brave front was a cold stream of despair. It caused them to shiver; then, from nowhere, Shaakhan roared with a voice of courage, it collapsed their fears and mustered strength in them with an unbelievable energy. They engaged again with the canapians punching and cutting as far as they could.

The king and his magicians were at the palace searching for the right spell to break through the newly strengthened canapians and send them back to rest. They searched for ages and were still not able to come up with the right spell.

The king sat beside them and leaned against the wall but his mind was far from them and he sat thinking, 'How are my warriors fairing? Are they exhausted or what? How I wish in my own reign, the kingdom could be perfect, I wish I were e able to abolish the old laws of my father and free my people from their slavery. Will they forget the evil I've caused to them? Yes of course, if I conquer the god, my name will go down in history as the most powerful and brave leader who ever existed on this planet. In addition, my story will be told repeatedly to even the unborn of this kingdom as that of the king who conquered the god and brought his people back to happiness. Yes I can do this with the help of my magicians; a king who will conquer the god of war to free his people!' he thought. At one point, the magicians stopped, and gazed at him because of the way he was smiling, very lost from the activities they were engaged in. They focused, watching him and the king himself did not realise it and kept on in his excitement and wishes. They turned and gazed at each other quizzically then, one of the magicians tapped him.

'Sir, you seem to be stressed, perhaps the woes of the kingdom are driving you insane,' said the magician.

'Have I done something nasty?' asked the king

'We're stunned seeing you sitting and smiling in the middle of...'

'Yes,' he gazed at them with passion and continued 'Have you ever thought of sleeping in the comfort of your bed, breathing the fresh air of nature, walking and seeing your people smile genuinely because you have given them a reason to; their freedom and their right to live freely and be whom they want to be?'

'Sir, for some time now we have watched you worried about how you would want the kingdom to be and we share in your faith; but sir, one thing at a time, the kingdom is under the attack of the god we all fear, we need courage and...'

'Exactly my magicians, exactly, if you saw me smiling as you claim, then I was under the throb of my imaginations, to see Krurice fall. Tomorrow, I will join the warriors north of Duce to fight alongside with them. I want to kill Krurice myself declaring victory over the gods and lead my people to a more certain future.' said the king. His words stunned the magicians and they opened their mouth wide. The king looked at them and they smiled and went back to searching for the right spells and enchantments to use against Krurice, reading every magical book found in the secret library of the kingdom.

A loud screech echoed in their ears - the voice of Zalinda, they ran to see him in his cradle but he was in an untouchable state; his eyes burning green. A sense of danger, the magicians thought and looked at each other warily readying their hands to quickly remove their wands and daggers if need arises. Like a snake, Zalinda crawled down his cradle and went towards the window holding the frame to support himself. A cup was on the floor next to the right leg of the last magician, Zalinda used his eyes and mushed the cup, then looked straight in to his eyes. There was a connection but the king did not notice it, only those with magic understood what he had done. In fact, he had discovered the right spell and enchantment to use and capture Krurice in his dream while he was sleeping. The magicians took note of the cup he squashed and went back to the book of black magic they had been reading all day and opened the 'can spell' and read it for themselves, then smiled and went to Zalinda and bowed to him. He had indeed has given them a solution to a long problem. They immediately told the king and explained to him the strategy they would use to succeed in destroying the god of war and end the suffering of the people of Duce.

Zalinda was just eleven months old, when he stretched his hand forward and a staff of thirty centimetres appeared on his hand. He used it to support himself and went to battle with the magicians together with the king. At the battlefield, the magicians knew the extent of his powers and did not take him for granted. They walked behind him. A frustrated canapian crossed his path and he savagely beat it with the powers of his staff and slammed him down the floor. His eyes glowed brightly and flames appeared from nowhere and consumed the body. Then, he led them to an oak tree, they stood there circling the tree and the magicians removed a black book of magic. Zalinda stretched forth his hand, and the head of the magician removed his dagger and cut through his thumb. The blood that oozed was collected in their goblet. Then from inside their secret sacks, they removed a powerful ancient mandrake root, mixed it with secret herbs, added it on to the goblet and enchanted it with a strong spell. The cup bubbled and the powers billowed from the cup in a thick dark cloud. The wind spread it apart and it went to every corner of the kingdom penetrating and destroying the canapians. Only the roaring noise of pain could be heard as they were crushed to dust. Krurice could not believe the type of powers he was feeling. Like a shadow, Zalinda appeared before him holding his staff right up, and struck the ground with it. The spell he released from his staff was stunning and Krurice looked warily from left to right tensed by the presence of Zalinda. Again they've met and his powers seemed to have tripled. By telepathy, Krurice communicated to Zalinda he would rather die by his own enchantment than die by the plunge of his magic. Krurice stood at one end and Zalinda stood at the other end contemplating, the king and the magicians came and met him. his eyes burnt again as he enchanted the king's sword and it glinted. The magicians told the king to strike the head of Krurice and immediately he did and Krurice fell down on the floor and died. All the canapians fell on the floor too and returned to their graves and the land became peaceful 'The rancid canapians are gone,' they said to one another, and Shaakhan raised his sword and they shouted aloud for their victory. All the canapians in Duce and the four kingdoms had been destroyed and the king and his magicians went back to the palace feeling happy. This was one of his best days and his innermost wish had been fulfilled. Standing outside the palace, one could hear the king giggling. The messenger came and announced to the king their victory; he jumped up as though he knew nothing and sent for his warriors to come home. When they arrived, the happiness on their faces was very pleasing and the king joined them and congratulated them. He declared twenty years of feast to celebrate their liberation.

At once, he changed the laws, virgins were no longer used for sacrifices. All were free to live a life that represented them - a phase of democracy and the indigenes of Duce were more than happy. Before their own eyes, they saw the odds of the kingdom and they were even.

His victory over the god quieted the secret warriors of the four kingdoms who were planning to attack Duce and take back their pride by defeating the kingdom.

'How can we go to war with a man who fought and defeated the god?' they thought and stayed low.

The king's victory had reached the Dwarf land, east of the four kingdoms. Their god Babran whom like Krurice was a demander of souls to protect the people, knew if he stayed quiet, the people may one day revolt against his wishes. He went and told their queen to attack the land of Duce avenging the death of Krurice. He told her that, they were now a threat to the Dwarf land since they wanted to capture every kingdom. At once, the queen heeded his word and they assembled their knights, which the god Babran fortified and led to the land of Duce to fight and conquer the kingdom. They travelled by sea with their boats, came and rested in one the four kingdoms where they camped. When the secret warriors of the four kingdoms heard about the arrival of the knights of Dwarf land, they went to attack them; they thought they wanted to attack their land.

'We come in peace,' said the commander of the knights looking with focus in to the eyes of the chief of the secret warriors. He did not say anything at first, his sword held firm, then he turned and looked at the rest of his warriors and asked,

'What's your mission?' asked the chief in command of the secret warriors of the four kingdoms.

'to crush the kingdom of Duce, we know how much you've wished to capture them; we want you people to form an alliance with us, join forces with us so that we can capture the kingdom and make them your slaves.' said the commander

'Very well spoken,' said the chief in command of the secret warriors and he stretched his arm and the commander stretched his and they greeted arm to arm accepting each other. When they had finished speaking to each other, a screech echoed in their ears, they turned around and saw no one. The chief of the secret warriors of the four kingdoms turned and said,

'Show yourself,' with his sword pointing to the open sky. They all looked at the sky warily darting end to end and around each other. A powerful breeze blew and Babran appeared before them.

'Babran!' The knights called out, the secret warriors knew not Babran. They had never heard of him and they held their swords firm and ready to defend themselves pushing their butts behind with their chests ahead. The knights bowed to Babran and they stood looking at them. The commander spoke to him.

'Our god, the protector of our land.'

They too bowed before Babran. They have never seen a creature like him; even the canapians were more beautiful than the god Babran.

'Are the gods always ugly or is that just the way they loved to appear to scare us the humans? Those who saw Krurice never said anything better about his beauty.' thought one of the warriors. Babran perceived his thoughts and unlike a chameleon, he didn't just change his colour but his entire physiology to look more of human and spoke to them, with a thunderous voice.

'I'll lead you all in spirit to capture the king of Duce and massacre the people of Duce for the sacrilege they've committed. I want to punish them and make them know that, without gods there are no humans.' said Babran and he fortified the secret warriors of the four kingdoms. The warriors fed them in secret and they were to attack Duce kingdom on the fourth night. The aftermath of his transformation numbed them and they stayed silently just waiting to take orders from him.

A week before the attack, they took a map of Duce and started planning their strategies to attack the kingdom using both manpower and magic. Their god was on their side.

There was always a connection when magic was involved and the aggressiveness of their plans to cause a massive havoc in the land of Duce echoed in the ears of Zalinda via telepathy. He was asleep; he shook and cried loudly throughout the night, something he had never done before. His mother came to him and sang him a beautiful lullaby-an ancient cradle song. Still, he wouldn't stop. His mother was surprised; it was his favourite song that sometimes caused his eyes to glow with love. Today was different, something was wrong, he woke his father and he lifted him up and tried to coddle, cuddle and play with him. He still would not stop crying and his cry disturbed everybody in the palace. He cried continuously for two days and the king summoned the magician to look in to Zalinda and explain. They searched through his heart with their sorcery but could see nothing. The magicians took him to their temple to search him more. After several attempts, they could see nothing and, only one day was left for the Knights and secret warriors of the four kingdoms to raid the land. They were much closer. He could not speak, his eyes burned yellow and glowed reflecting it to the eyes of the magicians. From it, they were able to read the mind of Zalinda. At once, they informed their king.

'In a few hours, the kingdom would be under attack by the Dwarfs,' said the magicians

'The dwarfs,' repeated the king.

'Yes sir,' 'What do they want? We have no dispute'

'Sir, Babran, the god of Dwarf land wants to revenge the death of Krurice for his people to be confident and keep on trusting him.'

'Could there be a link between this and Zalinda's cries?' asked the king

'Yes sir, indeed his cries were a premonition; it took time for us to see through his heart and read what was inside. We have less time sir,' said the magicians.

'Very well,' the king replied and dismissed himself from their midst, leaving them in quandary. He stood in his chamber for some time and he called Shaakhan. He came and bowed before him.

'You sent for me my lord,'

'Yes most honoured warrior, arise' the king said dabbing his sword on both of his shoulders.

'You do not look happy my lord, from your face I can tell there is something you have not yet revealed.' said Shaakhan

'Indeed, it is so; the kingdom is again under attack.'

'Attack?!''Sorry my lord for the rude interruption, I pray not your reprimand.'

'There is no time for formalities, I'm unable to see, my eyes are blinded with woes. Babran, the god of the Dwarf land wants to revenge for the killing of Krurice.' said the king as he pressed his eyes hard with his hand and wisely wiped out the tears away not to be seen. There was no time for emotions. 'Why Duce?' they thought, just when their kingdom was back to light. They were so worried, how many lives will be lost this time? From their research, Babran was not an easy god to joke with, compared to him, Krurice was just a joke. He was a god who could do anything for anything he desired and this time, he desired to see the fall of Duce, to trample on them for what they did, killing their god, which to him was a silly mistake, one which he was not willing to take lightly. He is a god and wanted to set an example for other kingdoms to follow, not to venture in the same way Duce had done. They killed Krurice after he had seen them through wars and hard times.

Day after day, the warriors kept wake in their armour and weapons waiting for the knights of Dwarf land to approach, the knights were just at the boundaries of the land of Duce. The warriors were not sure of the strength they had. At the borders upon entering the kingdom of Duce, the god Babran appeared to them again.

'Hahaha, loyal servants of the blessed, today will be the day the kingdom of Duce will face my wrath; everyone will cry out but no one will be there to help them because of their foolishness.' He smiled and cast a spell on them again and they went in to the kingdom, passing through the Elms valley, south of Duce. The king had positioned his warriors at every strategic area in the land. From the top of the hills above the Elms, the warriors saw the enormous crowd of knights marching into the kingdom. They rolled over large rocks down the valley, which ran down, swept a chunk of knights and pressed them over. From the hills, they descended with full force, holding firm their swords and engaging in combat with the knights of Dwarf land.

The warriors of Duce were killed in their numbers, the forces of the knight were unbelievably too much to withstand. From within them, they mustered the last of their strength keeping to their code to die for the kingdom and raid the knights, and like the dust, they were swept and crushed in pieces. Out of five million soldiers Shaakhan sent to battle with the knights of Dwarf land, only seven thousand were left in just first day at war with the knights of Dwarf land. Night came and the knights of Dwarf land marched to the forest of Elms and camped there. They had lost only fifty of their men, pressed by the heavy rocks the warriors rolled on them. They were still left with enough warriors to crush the kingdom of Duce. Seven million of their knights were still left or maybe even more but they were still massive like the human hair, may be uncountable. The warriors quickly retreated solidly to the terrace eight miles from the Elms and rested there, sending a messenger to the king to tell him how strong the knights of Dwarf land were. The message intimidated the king's sense of self, he supported his hand on his thrown and sat on his chair with his hand on his jaw and his small finger touching his lips slightly. All were confused, the people stood desperately in front of their king's palace to know the of the king's decision.

They were determined to see the kingdom fall, the magicians stood not because they wanted to but because of the frustration they were engaged in. The god Babran somehow had managed to hack in to their sorcery fizzling some of their powerful spells. They needed someone to help

170

them, someone powerful, someone who was but a child, Zalinda. A child that would in time be upheld as a true god. His powers were beyond human imagination. He has been to the dark world, the planet of gods where everyone was immortals and back. His decision to come down and save the people of Duce dated back when they were in slavery, under the captivity of the four kingdoms, battered and ill-treated, tormented, and in agony, they requested for someone powerful to save them, he came in deceit fooled them into sacrificing their love ones to in turn receive protection. For fifty years, the indigenes were forced to die premature deaths, for the sake of the kingdom and they knew nothing about it, not until the birth of Zalinda. The magician called out in fury; being passionate of their kingdom was falling.

'Zalinda! Son of the king, redeemer of our fatherland, arise and save your people,' like lightning, his eyes burned in flashes, his spirit awakened, he rose from his cradle, walked down and stood in front of the castle. The magicians ran close to him, mimicking what he did. No one feared him at this time for who he is but trusted in him to save them from their crisis. They had how he displayed in the time of the canapians and there was no doubt of his powers.

Zalinda once again was in control leading the magicians to war. From within his mind, he spoke to the magicians, telling them to send for the warriors of the kingdom to appear before him. They quickly told the king and he sent for them and they appeared before him. he told the magicians to lower their sacks and when they did, he dipped his hand in their various sack, removed a magic piece of chalk and drew a magic circle where he stood, sprinkled magical powder on it, then enchanted. The powers of his enchantment stimulated the winds and they rustled the trees with complete force, hitting them from one end to the other enough to make the trees angry, but they were without choice, their f magic was at work and the weakness of their anger could barely even be heard due to the strong magic. Another force was in the kingdom, threatening to chop every human in the kingdom, his eyes burned violently, and darkness emerged from the opened blue cloud. At once, thunder struck and lightening sparked, and, rain threatened to fall. Magic from his eyes sparked in to flames and put the circle ablaze, the magicians raised their heads to the heavens carrying their hands up with a complete confidence of fulfilment.

He sat down with his knees crossed and crushed the powerful mandrake roots, aloe Vera plant, and the auk in a platter and mixed it with a strange concoction until it was homogenous. He dipped his hand, scooped some of the mixture, rubbed between his palms and one by one he dabbed the shoulders of all the remaining warriors, including Shaakhan. The powers made their way into their soul fortifying them and making them immune to the knights of Dwarf land. He rose from his position and took a deep breath. The king joined them at the ritual and he was fortified too, preparing them all for the worst to come.

Babran had not felt any other powers above his or of the same equivalence and kept on doing just what pleased him because he knew the people of Duce were not a problem to him. Before night falls he must have crushed them down, he thought. His greatest challenged remained to visit the shrine of Krurice and hallow it. After four hours of intense incantation, he finally discovered the route to the shrine of krurice that the people had abandoned. He passed through the tunnel of Elms walking right down to Ebowa, centre of Duce near the shrine where Krurice died. He hallowed it and enchanted then collected earth from the shrine and took along with him to the place where his knights were and blew it over them; releasing another magical power to help them in battle with the Duce warriors.

The skirmishes grew tense, Zalinda had finished with his rituals and the king, Shaakhan and the magicians led the people to war riding on their horses back to the Elms valley to engage with the knights of Dwarf land. As they arrived, the knights picked up their swords, held them firm and ran towards them fighting with each other. 'Their strength was greater than when they first attacked them,' they noted. With the powers given to them, they fought like wild animals and killed all the knights of the Dwarf land including the secret warriors of the four kingdoms. Zalinda himself had left them and went ahead to engage with Babran, he looked at him closely and carefully wondering what a child could be doing alone in the lonely place he stood.

A secret voice echoed like a thunder into his mind.

'Who do you call a child, Babran?' there was a connection and the voice of his mind teleported strictly into his. Babran went into a trance for a few seconds to see through the person of Zalinda,

'A sorcerer! Boy, how did you get your powers?' he asked after using his magic to identify Zalinda. He did not wait to learn more of him but tried to challenge him. He conjured his staff, which appeared, in his hand, and he used it to wove his spell and cloak himself from being seen by Zalinda. From inside the spell, he flushed his magic, which beat Zalinda hard. He fell and woke up quickly retaliating, breaking through his spell. His eyes burned, his magicians appeared and used their wands to perform a spell that burnt the god and killed him. The few knights of the Dwarf land who were lucky to be alive were taken to the king. He kept them in prison. Another massive defeat has yet again been seen in the land of Duce and they were very happy. The king and the rest of the crew went back to the palace. He was impressed with them and he threw a party for them after they had mourned the warriors who had died in battle.

Chapter 12

'Shaakhan!' the king called out aloud

'Yes my lord,' he replied running towards him.

'Have you been able to get any useful information from them?' asked the king curiously.

'No sir.'

'What?!' the king questioned in fury.

'They are stubborn, my lord,' said Shaakhan looking carefully at the king.

'Give them some food,' said the king, Shaakhan left the king, collected the key to the prison from the palace guards and descended down two floors underneath the palace where the prisoners were kept. He walked to them; they were in chains and some hung on the cross with their amour and helmets covering their faces like a mask. They were the knights of Dwarf land to whom the king had shown mercy and spared their lives. Shaakhan walked to them and got them well tortured for them to reveal the secret of their land-their code that they used to invade them. They kept quiet and refrained from giving information concerning their land. He continued raising his whip made of thick steel, whacking at strategic points, which their armour could not cover leaving them with injuries and heavy bleeding.

When he was satisfied with the torture he had given them, he walked to each of them and removed their helmets one after the other until he reached the last person. She was Salina; he pulled it with anger to quickly remove the helmet.

'Salina! 'He called out. At once, she spat on her face, it was an insult to him and he retaliated with a backhand slap before repressing his emotions.

'What are you doing here? he asked, shocked. She was one of the girls he had nursed plans to marry but, her sister lost her virginity unlawfully and stole yams from the neighbours banner. she was reported to the king.- At the time they were in the dark world and she was beheaded by Shaakhan. He walked closer to her,

'You've not changed. I always thought of your beauty. Right now, you have betrayed the kingdom,' he spoke aloud in anger kicking in front of him a stool that was standing peacefully. Salina looked at him wickedly as if she should just eat him; unfortunately, she couldn't, she was in chains and even if they were to double her, she would not be able to scratch the nail of Shaakhan in battle not to talk of his flesh. Her mind was churn with anger bubbling and restless to tear him in pierces.

'I hate you and this bloody kingdom, why don't you just go ahead and finish me,' said Salina, trying to drag down her hurt arm, wincing in pain.

Shaakhan pretended as if he heard nothing and kept meandering - holding her hair firm and pulling it downward. It was painful but she was silent tightening her lips firmer and stiffening her body to resist the pain.

'Why don't you just kill me?' she snarled.

'No, no, not yet' he touted, 'if only the law hadn't been changed!'

'You are quite lucky,' he growled trying to intimidate her and forcing her words in a gruff manner to be heard. Then he calmed down and continued;

'You know, I could never have imagined that you could be the one to lead our enemies to destroy our blessed land' he stopped abruptly, gazed at the ceiling and gave her another slap, then left to tell the king about her tooting as he walked up the stairs.

'My lord' he called the king's attention. He was sitting on his decorated thrown in the palace inside his wide reception chamber.

'Speak on, sir Shaakhan of Duce' he said looking at him with focus

'One of our own joined force and fought us. Lady Salina, daughter of the palace nanny was amongst the knights of Dwarf land we captured at the battle field at Elms.'

'Bring her here to me' the king uttered and his face twisted with horror swaying around his thrown restlessly. The guards stood at attention watching at him in perpetual silence. A stray fly wandered into the palace and made its way into the king's left nostril. It began tickling him but the anger in him backed off his interest to pass out a deep breath that would send the fly out, the fly kept spinning around his nostril in confusion. The irritation reached its peak and unconsciously, the king sneezed loudly. One of his guards who stood directly at his right hand shook and fell on the ground and quickly woke up to take his position. Laughter choked their throats but they dared not and fastened their mouth so as not to release the laughter when the king was angry. The king looked at them, and went and sat on his seat. The king was furious that a child of the soil could betray the land. But, there was nothing more he could do, the law had been changed, the time where he ordered criminals of his kind to be beheaded were gone and he had sworn never to behead or kill any virgin in the land of Duce.

Shaakhan went down to the second floor underground and loosened Salina, pushing her forward to the direction of their king. She tripped on one of the stairs and fell roughly hurting her leg, Shaakhan pulled her up quickly and pushed her forward.

'Walk faster,' he forced

Salina was under pressure limping quickly to the direction she was dragged to. Shaakhan pushed her ahead again and she fell on the floor for a while before standing on her feet, he continued until they reached the presence of the king. Shaakhan forced her to kneel before the king. As the king rose from his seat, a fine bright light shone in from outside of the palace and reflected its rays into the ward; the king looked up for thirty seconds without a word gazing at her.

'I'm told you are Salina,' the king uttered

'Yes my lord,' she replied, looking at the king. The king took a deep breath, and went and sat again in his seat,

'How could you ally yourself with our enemies to raid the kingdom? Are you not ashamed of yourself, to kill and destroy your own comrades of your fatherland?'

'Take her away, and hang her on the cross outside,' the king ordered. Shaakhan took her and instructed his warriors to do as the king had said. She was hung outside in the open where only the sky and the vegetation were her friends. She would stay there for seven days in the cold before taken back into the prison.

Two weeks later, the king planned to attack the Dwarf lands and to rule over the territory. He invited Salina in the palace to get information from her; she knew nothing concerning them except the fact that she had seen their god Babran. The king returned her back to prison. The king knew little about the Dwarf land, he gathered his best geographers, they too knew very little. They sat calculating, confused on which route to best take and invade the Dwarf land. They sat contemplating, when one of the geographers, Simon Kris, opted,

'I have an idea; we can take an underground route leading to the Dwarf land, I've been there once.'

'Are you certain?'

'Certainly my lord,' he replied keeping a closer watch at their gaze, darting at the map in front of him,

'Here sir,' he said pointing at the map, 'north of the four kingdoms entering through south, between the two regions is a mossy mountain, we could camp at the valley and regain our strength before invading.'

'Very well,' the king nodded

'Shaakhan, prepare the warriors, in two days we shall attack the Dwarf land.'

'Yes sir,' he answered and left to his home, dressed in his military attire and went to the camp and assembled the warriors telling them the plan at hand.

They prepared their cargo, arranged their carriages and prepared their horses for the journey to Dwarf land. The two days the king had given them to prepare elapsed. Shaakhan, the magicians and the geographer led the warriors through the underground route, heading north of the four kingdoms, until they came to rest at the valley after the mossy mountain just before entering the Dwarf land. At night as they were asleep, funny creatures with cranky-long fingers and thick tattered scabrous fleshy body supported by a skeletal leg descended from the mountain to where they had camped. They had blue eyes and walked in paliforms. Shaakhan was sleeping right at the foot of the mountain; it came closer to him, and touched Shaakhan. He was shocked and screamed-gripping his sword. The rest of the warriors woke up and held their swords firm ready to defend their selves. The creature screeched, and jumped on Shaakhan's body holding his hand and biting a large area. He flicked his hand here and there shouting for help. The other warriors jumped in front, came closer to him and cut the creature across its body before pulling it off Shaakhan's hand. It had managed to chop off a large portion of flesh from his body and he winced in pain. The magicians quickly removed from inside their sack a powerful herb, crushed it and then applied it on the position, the blood immediately stooped oozing and they tied the injured region with pieces of cloth they tore from their garment.

Simon was scared, so were the rest of them but he managed to croak,

'Please be silent not to wake their multitude, it seems they are somewhere in the caves on the other side of the mountain, these creatures are dangerous.'

'How come you never told us about these creatures?' asked Shaakhan in fury.

'I've read books about them, but the book described their location as west, I never thought we shall come in contact with such carnivorous creatures here at the south.' said Simon

One of the magicians walked closer to him too and asked.

'How well do you know these creatures?'

'According to ancient scholars, these creatures turn into vultures during the day and at night they turn in to what we just saw. They call them Khaleans; they always pass through the west and hunt humans from the Dwarf lands, just like Duce, they prayed to their god to save them from the hands of these dreadful predators. Babran came from the planet of the gods and opted to protect them but in return, they were to sacrifice annually a virgin to him.'

'Ahh! Wait... we killed their god, so the kingdom is left loose for the Khaleans to attack and hunt humans at will?'

'Of course, the powers of Babran scared them away, maybe, the reason why they made this place their habitat.' said Simon

They turned and looked at each other warily, then, Shaakhan spoke to them,

'These people are our enemy, yes we wouldn't forget but at the same time their safety remains in our hands. We should quickly march into Dwarf land and protect them from these creatures. We have killed their god and they remain vulnerable and need us. I'm sure Babran forced them into war with us; they had no choice if they were to continue being protected.

For the kingdom,' said Shaakhan

'For the kingdom and for our king.' They raised their swords up and marched up, climbing the mountains and entered Dwarf land. The place was silent and solitary, scattered with human parts and corpses and a thin cloud, which wonders just above their heads. To the left, they could hear the birds singing songs of sorrow and the few animals who had survived stood numb watching at them parading the land of hopelessness. They stood gazing at the land in pity walking from one region to the other searching for survivors, tracking each footstep they saw and following it till the end. Maybe to another dead body or barely another frustrated animal straying aimlessly, until the morning was nigh. They left and rested at the foot of mount Eboa, a small mountain in Dwarf land. They relieved themselves, putting down their loads, draining the water in their boots and airing their feet. Far to the right, a group of warriors stood sharpening their swords and arrows. On the left, other warriors stood discussing, the magicians were somewhere at the top of the mountain, reading their books of spells. Some warriors were just so tired, resting on top of bamboos that they had made into bed, It didn't take long, the ground started vibrating,

'What's happening?' they asked one another touching down their palms to feel the vibration,

'Back off, arm yourselves' Shaakhan cautioned and they seized their swords from whatever position they had kept it and held it firm preparing themselves against any attack. Suddenly, voices started echoing in their ears, the magicians ran down from the top of the mountain with their wands firmly in place.

'Show yourself' some uttered leaning forward with swords in their hands, only a slow whisper could be heard from every corner,

'Can you guess what it is?'

'May be the Khaleans, Simon told me that they are very good at sniffing the scent of humans,'

'Hmm, I'm scared,'

'Stop being a coward, it is our destiny to fight and conquer. Where have you kept your manners?'

As their words echoed, bright sunrays shone in their direction. Long shadows of something they were not seeing very well appeared to be emerging from under the ground at the side of the mountain, they squinted using their hands to shelter their eyes and looking focus with their swords firm.

'Ready for attack, Shaakhan said hoping it was the Khaleans. The shadows seemed to be approaching and he gave orders,

'Attack,'

They ran towards the shadows and started pulling themselves backward.

'Humans, some actually survived?' they were scared and Shaakhan walked to them, 'We heard your tragedy and we came to render our own support'

'Very well,' said the Dwarf land Queen, 'where are you from?'

They looked at each other intensely.

'Duce'

'Duce?!' they backed off removing their own swords. The few knights left immediately surrounded their queen, the warriors too adjusted.

Shaakhan spoke, 'We've come to save you.' Still, the queen did not believe them and she gazed at them mistrustfully. Shaakhan lowered his sword and stood straight; the queen walked in the middle of the knights and spoke to the warriors of Duce

'I do not know what your mission is but if you've come to help us fight the Khaleans, the most dangerous and feared creatures in Dwarf land, I welcome you.' He marched forward, they looked at each other for few seconds and greeted arm to arm. The rest of the crowd clapped, the loudness of their noise woke the Khaleans and they transformed in to vultures and flew in to Dwarf land some hundred metres from where they were uniting. The queen pulled her sword from its case and was just about raising it up. At once, Shaakhan pulled his own sword to defend himself,

'Look behind you,' he walked backwardly for some few centimetres then turned to look at what the queen had pointed.

'The Khaleans,' he shouted. They all adjusted but in fact, he had thought the queen wanted to engage in combat with him. No one trusted the other and they decided to be friendly enemies to fight a common enemy. The Khaleans flew in their midst, they gave gap facing the khaleans with courage. Before their eyes, the khaleans chugged closer to one of the warrior of Duce and pierced his eye, bursting it. The rest of the warriors attacked defending him, passing him inside the crowd for treatment. The vultures were so eager and fearless to continue eating the humans. The magicians suddenly pushed forward, using their wands, they ridiculed the

Khaleans to know their ability. It meant nothing to them, they kept on threatening to prey on them. The magicians didn't hesitate, they whooshed their spell to destroy them. The queen was busy fighting; she turned and saw that the magicians had cast a spell on the Khaleans.

'No!' she cried out

The Khaleans had stood still shrugging and struggling to take the form the warriors first encountered them at the valley.

'What?' Shaakhan questioned

The queen gave no answer, stood numb gazing at their ugly transformation. Their legs froze at the spot and they were unable to move, the beast in them fully emerged, their cranky long fingers suddenly developed this time with thorns on it. They made a loud noise, their friends came from all corners of the Dwarf land and before they knew it, they were in their millions looking very hungry. The magicians tried another spell and cast it on them but it seemed almost meaningless because it did not affect them in any way. The queen walked to them,

'These creatures and magic are two sides of the coin, your spell just helped them to build their form. According to ancient stories, these creatures were very friendly but because their own form, were very scary, they did not want to scare the humans. They went to an ancient sorcerer, the most powerful wizard the world has ever had, to convert them be like humans, if not for all the time, then for a day so that when they go to sleep, their bodies can go back to their alien form. He accepted and instead used his magic to turn them in to vultures. They never knew, that night, they walked and stood in nearby forests close to the Dwarf land waiting that, the day should show up so that they could be transformed into humans able to socialise with them. They instead turned into vultures and their looks angered them. They grew furious, the love they had for humans collapsed and they trampled on the sorcerer. He thought he could use his magic to eliminate them but forgot that the spell he had cast on them was powerful and only helped them to absorbed other magic to rebuild themselves, making them more dangerous. They killed the sorcerer and invaded the Dwarf land eating and destroying humans till this date. Using your spell had just moved them to another level of wickedness, they hate sorcerers, and hate all humans.'

When she had finished explaining herself to the magicians, the Khaleans rolled in their midst, attacking them with rage. They killed the warriors in their numbers, all the magicians were killed as well-and fought day and night and the Khaleans kept on attacking.

Chapter 13

Back at the palace, the princess was feeding Zalinda. Suddenly he coughed out the food that was in his mouth and wriggled violently wincing in pain. His mother carried him and placed him on her shoulder, tapping his back gently and pampering him. That was not what he wanted and it annoyed him the more, he wriggled with force and fell off from her mother's hand. He did not cry as she would expect. She lifted him up and laid him in his bed. He covered his eyes as if gone to sleep, and enchanted in his heart.

'*Cshiageh aleah nchow mbo leng'na-leng'na*' pronouncing every word with precision, only his lips shook but the voice was silent. At once, a rainbow appeared somewhere in the open cloud. The cloud broke in pattern taking his form. From it the seven angels of ancient wizards left, whishing down to his cradle and took his soul straight to the battlefield passing through wonderlands and across the horizon and gleamed at Dwarf land. He was invincible and used his magic to strengthen the warriors and they fought with excessive energy. They themselves were surprised where such energy was from; killing and defeating the Khaleans, he left them and returned to his body. They went tired and famished but indeed, they had procured victory. The queen was very happy, she took them into her palace. Her people fed them, they drank and ate to satisfaction, and the next day, they rose and to rode home.

'What will you tell your king?' she questioned

'I'll tell him what happened to us, what we've done.'

'Very well, go in peace' she waved at them as they left. The Dwarf land indigenes lives' had been spared and the intention of crushing the kingdom of Duce left their mind. Shaakhan noted the way the queen looked at him and suspected some veins of emotions even though she did not make it clear, he could see it from her eyes.

Arriving home, the king was happy to meet them and embraced them seeming very excited. Shaakhan walked forward and told the king what had taken place in the Dwarf land and how he decided to spare the lives of the poor few who were left. The king's smile gradually faded and was replaced by a cold look that makes his muscles tight and stiff. The veins of his eyes stretched above limit and blood pumped across turning it red. He forcefully swallowed the bunch of saliva that rested at the back of his palate and you could see it tearing its way down his gut. He gave Shaakhan a wicked look and said.

'On whose orders was your decision based?'

'Against all odds, my lord, I have failed you by disobeying your orders, I'm not worthy of your trust.' said Shaakhan.

'Very well spoken, very well said, for twenty years you've served me right from the time of my father when I was a prince. You saved me on many occasions and I decided to break the warrior's code and promoted you from my manservant to my most trusted commander of my warriors because I trusted you. I saw the braveness in you to carry out my bidding. This one circumstance of your disobedience has made you unworthy. If the kingdom is entrusted in your care, you will betray them, I look at you with disdain but I cannot forget what you have done for the kingdom. However, I'll grant you some clemency for breaking the warrior's code and breaking the laws of your land. You are banished from the kingdom and by nightfall, no man or woman of this land should sniff your scent. Farewell servant of the kingdom but

I uphold the law and as your king I am meant to protect this land.' Said the king

Shaakhan stood gazing at the king, confused on what to do or say and wobbled his mouth without any word being uttered; he had lived all his life in Duce, he was confused of where to go. He went to his chamber, told his wife, packed all his belongings and loaded them in his carriage.

'Shaakhan, Shaakh...,' he had no time for her, he was packing his belongings, 'Shaakhan listen to me.' said the princess

'I have no time for words,' said Shaakhan in fury

'I can speak to my father about this,' said the princess

'My wife, hold your breath. I know the king your father, the most he did was granting me this clemency; nothing in the world can convince him to withdraw his word. It was not personal, he took it in the court before his officials and the warriors of the land. So, telling me you will influence him to change his mind is like saying the fish will leave the water and live on land with humans. I know I will never see you again, I know I will never see my son. When he grows up, please tell him about his father, who he was. Goodbye my love, goodbye my son,' and he kissed the air and went into his carriage and rode off. The king had sent some of his warriors to escort him to the boundaries. The princess stood weeping, Zalinda looked at his father and tears ran down his cheek as he waved to his father, supporting himself on the window gazing at his father until all of him had disappeared. Then, he crept back to his mother. At the palace, the king himself felt very bad and sad but it was a lesson.

The princess was sad and angry with her father, and the news of Shaakhan's exile reached the ears of the people right up to the four kingdoms. They now know he has been sacked from his duty. The secret warriors who were the rebels of the four kingdoms, went to the borders and hid there waiting for Shaakhan. When the king's escort had returned, Shaakhan was left alone in the forest entering the Damland, east of Brooks and central to the four kingdoms. Spears from nowhere, shot by unknown person, pierced through the ground. He raised his head up and saw the rebels. He removed his sword and they went closer to him, and surrounded him and engaged him into a fight. He was alone and they fought him tearing through him and cutting him hazily. He was weak after bleeding heavily; they approached him, cut his head, and took with them in their kingdom. They placed it on a stick and danced round it rejoicing.

Chapter 14

Six months after Shaakhan's death, Zalinda was not himself and from time to time, he kept glancing at his mother with pity. One afternoon, he spoke out and enchanted; a curse flew on to the king, his body bath with blood and the souls of the people he had killed kept appearing to him. He went insane and ran out of the palace. The guards chased him, and he ran and kicked his leg on the root of an oak tree and fell into an open well, which was twenty-five metres deep. Before the guards could struggle to remove him, he was already dead; they brought him before the people and gave him a befitting burial. The angels of darkness appeared and flushed their spells killing everybody in the palace but Zalinda had seen his mother's heart through her tears that constantly dripped into his eyes. He knew she was a true woman of modesty, someone who has the best interests of the people at heart, a mother to be their queen and the saviour to the people of Duce. He absorbed the spell that was cast on her and took it to himself and spared his mother's life, he reverted the prophecy and let her live. Zalinda took his own live with his enchantment. The princess finally became queen, she grieved for some days and the elders of the land took her to the secret chamber and inaugurated her as the queen of the Duce.

The people were happy, she modified the laws again and they were introduced with a new form of life - democracy. She closed the page of fallacy and myth.. A true democratic generation, she restored the pride of the four kingdoms and their sovereignty, and she created relationship with them and they went into business. The land was enchanted with songs of praise and anthems to hail their queen."